CONCORD FREE PRESS PRESENTS

10

A DECADE OF READING AND GIVING

Concord Free Press Presents

OUR 10TH ANNIVERSARY COLLECTION

CONCORD
FREE
PRESS

Published by Concord Free Press
152 Commonwealth Ave.
Concord, Massachusetts 01742

www.concordfreepress.com

Designed by Chris DeFrancesco

ISBN: 978-0-9908059-7-7

Printing of this book was subsidized by a generous donation from **Harvest** in New York City. (www.getharvest.com)

For you, generous reader.

Contents

IT'S SIMPLE. We publish great books and give them away to intrepid readers. In exchange, they donate to a cause of their choice or someone in need—then pass their book along. In our first decade, readers around the world have given more than $3 million to thousands of diverse organizations and people, going way beyond our wildest expectations when we started our *grand experiment in subversive altruism.*

The Concord Free Press works because our writers, editors, designers, proofreaders, and other contributors all volunteer their time and considerable talents for free. Together, we've created a revolutionary new publishing model, one that can transform words and stories into generosity and kindness.

In *Concord Free Press Presents*, you'll find work from writers of short stories, poems, novels, articles, memoirs, and more. All joined by a shared trait—a very big heart.

May theirs inspire yours.

—the Editors

The End of the World Is Not Nigh

KEVIN ASHTON

ALL OUR LIVES, people have been telling us we are just one catastrophe away from annihilation. Climate change is today's most common concern, but overpopulation, nuclear war, pandemics, and the rise of artificial intelligence are also popular. Whatever the cause, the hypothesis is always the same: some disaster will lead to an irreversible collapse of civilization quickly followed by the extinction of humanity.

These apocalyptic fears have less to do with the rise of robots, sea levels, or global temperatures than we might imagine. Every generation has believed the end of the world is nigh. Fear of apocalypse is innate and primal, a bit like fear of snakes. The number of stories we tell about the end of the world increases not with risk but with population: there is always about one apocalyptic prediction for every hundred million people on the planet. Fifteen widely publicized, specific extinction dates came and went in the nineteenth century, another fifty-nine passed in the twentieth century, and the twenty-first century is on track for at least eighty-four. There are also thousands of fictional accounts. The first apocalyptic novel was published in 1268, the first apocalyptic movie in 1916, and the first apocalyptic video game in 1988. As soon as we invent a new medium, we use it to tell tales about the end of the world. All these apocalyptic predictions and stories trigger our primal fear and make a big impression: worldwide, fourteen percent of people think the human race will become extinct in their lifetime. In the United States, the number is higher: twenty-two percent.

All these people are wrong. The claim that we are about to become extinct does not stand up to even a little critical thinking. Humanity will not die out in your lifetime nor anybody else's. The end of the world is not nigh.

This conclusion does not mean wishing away problems like climate change. Only a shrinking, aging minority still denies the obvious: climate change is a real problem created by us, and it is already causing disastrous fires and floods, deadly hurricanes, typhoons, and tidal waves, mass extinctions, crop failures, land erosion, terrible poverty in some places and unprecedented mass migration in others, and blowing on the coals of political extremism everywhere. Tens of millions of people will die of climate change. That is terrible, especially as their deaths could have been avoided completely, but it is not extinction. Climate change does not make the end of the world inevitable, imminent, or even likely. (The same is true of nuclear war, infectious disease, meteor strikes, and all the other horrors and catastrophes that apocalyptic prophets like to warn us about.)

One of the great misunderstandings about climate change is that the world will change so fast we will not have time to adapt. This may be based in part on confusion about the extinction of the dinosaurs. In the 1980s, scientists realized that the extinction of the dinosaurs was caused by a meteorite striking the earth. This led to some iconic images: on a vast plain, giant lizards, cud dangling from their slack dino-jaws, stare upward as a fiery meteorite smokes through the sky. When the meteorite lands, it explodes, bringing flames, shockwaves, rains of molten rock, and tidal waves which cause the dinosaurs' instant extinction. These images have helped shape what we imagine when we hear about environmentally-caused extinction from climate change, and they are completely wrong.

Yes, a meteorite with a six-to-nine-mile diameter struck the earth in what is now Mexico 6.6 million years ago. Yes, it caused tsunamis that reached inland more than 186 miles, triggered earthquakes that would have scored eleven or higher on Richter's magnitude scale, threw sulfur into the atmosphere that returned to earth as acid rain, damaged the ozone layer for several years, created huge dust clouds that made the days darker, and temporarily warmed the planet by one or two degrees. And yes, dinosaurs that were near the meteorite's point of impact, or within range of the tsunamis, or struck by debris from the earthquakes, were either killed instantly or mortally wounded. But these were a small fraction of all the total number of dinosaurs on the planet. All other dinosaurs survived the impact. Few if any species of dinosaur became extinct—or even got close to becoming extinct—on the day the meteorite fell. Dinosaurs did not become extinct until tens of thousands of years after the meteorite's impact. The extinction was only abrupt in geological time. In human time, it took forever. (Ten thousand years ago, we hadn't even invented agriculture.)

The extinction of most dinosaur species was caused by cascading changes in the food chain resulting from environmental changes that followed the impact. Many plants became extinct or did not grow as well, which led to less food for herbivores, which led to fewer and smaller herbivores for carnivores to eat. Most species of dinosaurs bred less, died younger, and their populations declined, generation by generation, until they eventually became extinct, one species at a time, at different times. Many species of theropod dinosaurs, a large sub-order of dinosaurs, survived the meteorite impact and evolved into birds. There are around 100 billion birds alive today, and about twice as many bird species as mammal species. The truth about dinosaur extinction is not only that it took tens of thousands of years, but also that many dinosaurs did not become extinct at all: some are singing outside your window, and you may be eating one of the others for lunch.

The most important factor in avoiding extinction during

massive environmental change is surviving long enough to adapt. And this is where humans have a unique advantage. In every other species, adaptation requires evolution. Evolution takes place gradually, generation by generation, and useful adaptations require hundreds or thousands of generations. But humans are different. We do not have to wait for natural selection to pick advantageous individual mutations, then spread them across the species. We adapt collectively, by consciously and deliberately creating better technology. When there was not enough warmth, we discovered fire; when there was not enough food, we created farms; when there was not enough water, we invented wells; and, generation after generation, we built a world of ever-improving tools that supplemented our biology, adjusted our environment, increased our fertility, extended our lifespans, and improved our odds of survival. Our entire population participates in and benefits from this process, and we can improve our technology countless times within a single generation. If the meteorite that killed off the dinosaurs landed today, it would be the greatest catastrophe in human history and we would lose hundreds of millions or maybe even billions of people, but the survivors would adapt by creating new and improved technology, would have many generations in which to do it, and our species would not only survive but also thrive. This is our greatest strength: we adapt by creating new tools, not by evolving new bodies.

One example is how we survived the bubonic plague. Plague, like climate change, is an environmental reaction to new technology. Plague is caused by a bacterium called *Yersinia pestis* that lives in fleas that live on black rats. For thousands of years, *Yersinia pestis* was native to a largely unpopulated part of western China, and it mainly infected small mammals, not humans. Then, about ten thousand years ago, after we invented agriculture, we started developing trade routes and improving our transportation technology. The black rats, which normally only travel a few hundred meters in one lifetime, stowed away on our new forms of transport, particularly ships, traveling hundreds or thousands of miles and spreading plague all over the world.

The first plague pandemic started in 540, moving along the shores of the Mediterranean in sail boats and oar-powered galleys used to transport wheat around the Roman Empire; it killed ten percent of the world's population.

The second plague pandemic started in 1346. Ships had transformed since the first pandemic: oars were set away from hulls in stands called outriggers, which allowed them to be longer and generate more power; decks had been added, creating cargo holds; rudders had gone from upright paddles to powerful, streamlined steering systems capable of turning heavy boats without creating drag; compasses made it easier to navigate; cranes made it easier to load and unload cargo; and sails were no longer triangles pointing forward, but squares rigged across the wind. These changes made ships larger, faster, able to carry more, capable of traveling either without wind or straight into it, and suitable for long voyages over rough seas from the Mediterranean to the north of Europe. These new ships took the second plague, which became known as the Black Death, farther and faster than the first plague, and it killed twenty percent of the world's population, around one hundred million people.

The third plague pandemic started in 1855, when ships were powered by steam, traveled around the world, and were fifty times larger and five times faster than the ships of the Middle Ages. This third plague was an extinction level threat; our new technology gave it the power to travel the world, decimate the human population, and cause the collapse of civilization. That did not happen, of course. We survived the third plague because of new technology.

Innovations in ship building and navigation led to an "Age of Discovery" between the 14th and 18th centuries, when Europeans invaded the Americas, Australia, New Zealand, and parts of Africa and Asia. This in turn caused an age of infectious disease in the 18th and 19th centuries because settler colonists and slavers unwittingly transported previously rare and unknown deadly bacteria and viruses all over the world. Plague was the most dangerous of these, but there was also cholera, which killed hundreds of thousands worldwide; typhus, which decimated Napoleon's army and killed over a hundred thousand people in Ireland; yellow fever, which killed tens of thousands in the United States and caused two presidents, George Washington and John Adams, and their governments to flee the then-capital, Philadelphia; smallpox, which killed 400,000 Europeans a year in the 18th century, ended the reigns of five monarchs and was a leading cause of death worldwide; dysentery, which killed 95,000 soldiers during the US Civil War; and epidemic meningitis, which first appeared in Geneva in 1805, then spread to New England and Africa.

At first, the rich, powerful, and political denied that these diseases were infectious because they did not want to lose money by closing ports and quarantining ships. They claimed sickness appeared spontaneously and was caused by "bad air." But, in the mid-1880s, as the third plague began spreading out of China, the truth started to become obvious. Louis Pasteur and Robert Koch showed that there were tiny organisms, or "germs," everywhere, and that in the right conditions these organisms would grow in population. Pasteur's initial experiments were in wine, beer, and milk, but he and Koch soon turned their attention to understanding anthrax in cows. As the plague approached Taiwan (then part of Japan), Koch discovered the bacteria that causes anthrax, Pasteur developed a vaccine to prevent cholera in chickens, and veterinarian Jean Joseph Henri Toussaint developed an anthrax vaccine. While Taiwan was succumbing to the plague, Pasteur started testing a rabies vaccine on humans and founded the first Pasteur Institute. In 1894, when the plague arrived in Hong Kong, two scientists working independently both discovered its bacterium:

Alexandre Yersin in Hong Kong; and Kitasato Shibasabur in Japan. Two years later, when the plague reached India, a Russian researcher working there named Waldemar Haffkine developed a vaccine and tested it on volunteers. By the end of 1899, four million Indians had been vaccinated with Haffkine's vaccine, and plague in India started to decline. Ten million Indians were killed, but that was only about one-third of one percent of India's population. In the same year, a French researcher named Paul-Louis Simond showed that plague bacteria were spread by fleas; then German scientists Paul Ehrlich and Alfred Bertheim, Japanese microbiologist Sahachir Hata, and others, started developing antibacterial medicines for various diseases, a class of drugs that came to be called "antibiotics." The third plague continued to spread along worldwide shipping routes for another fifty years, to Africa, Russia, San Francisco, South America, and the Caribbean; but, its impact was greatly limited by the new technology of vaccination, and then was all but ended by the development of an antibiotic for plague, which began in 1943 with the discovery of a bacteria called *Streptomyces griseus* in the soil of New Jersey by an American microbiologist named Albert Schatz. Because of all these discoveries, the third plague pandemic did not wipe out humanity; instead, it killed less than one percent of our population—most of them before vaccines were available. Today, only about six hundred and fifty people are infected with plague each year, and more than eighty percent of them survive, usually after being given antibiotics.

The story of the plague shows how we will deal with climate change, and all the other threats we will face after that. After frustrating and deadly periods of confusion, denial, and delay, we will make new discoveries and develop new technologies that will first mitigate then solve the problems, allowing us to survive and continue to thrive. A lifetime of listening to apocalyptic propaganda, in the form of predictions, prophesies, and dystopian stories, may have predisposed us to believe that the end of the world is nigh, but history is a far more reliable guide, and it shows us the opposite. We change our technology, which changes our environment, which leads us to change our technology. Humanity has a unique ability to create, invent, and discover, and it will allow our species to live forever.

The Happy Place

JOYCE CAROL OATES

PROFESSOR! HELLO.

White winter days, sunshine on newly fallen snow. You have come to the *happy place* for it is Thursday afternoon.

Another week, and you are still alive. Your secret you carry everywhere and so into the *happy place*.

So close to the heart, no one will see.

Not a happy season. Not a happy time. Not in the history of the world and not in the personal lives of many.

You wonder how many are like you. Having come to prefer dark to daylight. Sweet oblivion of sleep to raw wakefulness.

Yet: in the wood-paneled seminar room on the fifth floor of North Hall. At the top of the smooth-worn wooden staircase where a leaded window overlooks a stand of juniper pines. In the wind, pine boughs shiver and flash with melting snow. The *happy place*.

Here is an atmosphere of optimism light as helium. You laugh often, you and the undergraduates spaced about the polished table.

Why do you laugh so much?—you have wondered.

Generally it seems: the more serious the subjects, the more likely some sort of laughter.

The more intensity, the more laughter.

The more at stake, the more laughter.

The *happy place* is the solace. The promise.

Waking in the morning stunned to be *still alive*. The profound fact of your life now.

Already at the first class meeting in September you'd noticed her: *Ana*.

Of the twelve students in the fiction writing workshop it is *Ana* who holds herself apart from the others. From you.

When they laugh, Ana does not laugh—not often.

When they answer questions you put to them, when in their enthusiasm they talk over one another like puppies tumbling together—Ana sits silent. Though Ana may look on with a faint (melancholy) smile.

Or, Ana may turn her gaze toward the wall of windows casting a ghostly reflected light onto her face and seem to be staring into space—oblivious of her surroundings.

Thinking her own thoughts. Private, not yours to know.

You feel an impulse to lean across the table, to touch Ana's wrist. To smile at her, ask—*Ana, is something wrong?*

But what would you dare ask this girl who holds herself apart from her classmates? *Are you troubled? Unhappy? Distracted? Bored?*—not possible. One of the others in the seminar might take Ana aside to ask such questions, but you, the adult in the room, the Professor, don't have that right, nor would you exercise that right if indeed it were yours. Still less should you touch Ana's wrist.

It is a very thin wrist. The wrist of a child. So easily snapped! The young woman's face is delicately boned, pale, smooth as porcelain, her eyes are beautiful and thick-lashed but somewhat shadowed, evasive.

You have noticed, around Ana's slender neck, a thin gold chain with a small gold cross.

The little cross must be positioned just so, in the hollow at the base of Ana's throat, that is as pronounced and (once you have noticed it) conspicuous as your own.

(What is it called?—*suprasternal notch*. A physical feature aligned with thinness, generally conceded to be a genetic inheritance.)

Indeed, Ana is a very diminutive young woman. To the casual eye she would seem more likely fourteen than eighteen and hardly a *woman* at all.

Ana must weigh less than one hundred pounds. No more than five feet two. You see, without having actually noticed until now, that she wears loose-fitting clothing, a shapeless pullover several sizes too large, and the thought strikes you, unbidden, fleeting, that Ana may be acutely *thin*. Her diffident manner makes her appear even smaller. *As if she might curl up, disappear. Cast no shadow.*

How vulnerable Ana appears!—to gaze upon her is to feel that you must protect her.

Yet, you suppose that there are many who would wish to take advantage of her.

When the others speak of "religious belief"—"superstition"—with the heedlessness of bright adolescents wielding their wits like blades, Ana sits very still at her end of the table, eyes downcast. Touching the cross around her neck.

Why doesn't Ana speak, intervene? Defend her beliefs, if indeed she has beliefs?

Yes. This is a superstitious symbol I am wearing. What is it to you?

The discussion has risen out of the week's assignment, a short story by Flannery O'Connor saturated with Christian imagery and the mystery of the Eucharist, and Ana, like the others, has written an analysis of the story.

But Ana remains silent, stiff until at last the discussion veers in another direction. Glancing at you, an expression of— is it reproach? hurt?—for just an instant.

The *insomniac night* is the antithesis of the *happy place*.

Unlike the *happy place*, which is specifically set and unfortunately finite, as an academic class invariably comes to an end, the *insomniac night* has no natural end.

If you cannot sleep in the night, the night will simply continue into the next, sun-blinding day.

You have thought *Is she a refugee* for her spoken English is hesitant, imperfect. You have not wanted to think *Is she a victim. Has she been hurt. What is the sorrow in her face. Why is she so unlike the others.*

Ana's face, that seems wise beyond her years. (You are certain you are not misinterpreting.)

Oh, why does Ana not *smile?* Why is it Ana who alone resists the *happy place?*

In twenty-seven years of teaching you have encountered a number of *Ana's*—surely.

Yet, you don't recall. Not one. And why should you, students are impermanent in the lives of teachers. There is nothing profound in this situation. Ana has done adequate work for the course, she has never failed to hand in her work on time. You have no reason to ask her to come and speak with you, no reason at all.

Ana's reluctance (refusal?) to smile on cue, as others so easily smile—this is a small mystery.

Is it your pride that is hurt? But how little pride means to you, frankly.

You are conscious of the (unwitting) tyranny of the group. Of any group no matter how congenial, well-intentioned.

That all in the group laugh, smile, agree with the others, or "disagree" politely, or flirtatiously. The (unwitting) tyranny of the classroom that even the most liberal-minded instructor cannot fail to exert. *Pay attention to me. Pay attention to the forward-motion of the class. No silences! No inward-turning—this is not a Zen meditation. A small class is a sort of skiff, we are all paddling. We are all responsible for paddling. We are aiming for the same destination. We are aware (some of us keenly) of those who are not paddling. Those who have set their paddles aside.*

Perhaps Ana has not clearly understood that enrollment in a

small seminar brings with it a degree of responsibility for participation. Answering questions, asking questions. "Discussing." The workshop is not a lecture course: students are not expected to take notes. Perhaps it was an error in judgment for Ana to enroll in a course in which (it seems apparent) she has so little interest as, you are thinking, it was an error in judgment for you to accept her application, out of seventy applications for a workshop of twelve.

Why had you chosen Ana Fallas? A first-year student, with no background in creative writing? Something in the writing sample Ana had provided must have appealed to you, a glimpse of Hispanic domestic life perhaps, that set it aside from others that were merely good, conventional.

Though now, as it has turned out, Ana's work has seemed less exceptional. Careful, circumspect. Nothing grammatically wrong but—nothing to call attention to itself.

As if Ana is trying to make herself into one of *them*—the Caucasian majority. It is likely that Ana is intimidated by the university—its size, its reputation. By the other students in the writing class. She is but one of only two first-year students, and the other is Shan from Beijing, a dazzling prodigy intending to major in neuroscience.

The others are older than Ana, more experienced. Three are seniors, immersed in original research—senior theses. Most of them are Americans and those who are not, like Shan, and Ansar (Pakistan), and Colin (U.K.), have studied in the United States previously and seem to have traveled widely. Ana is the only Hispanic student in the class and (you are guessing) she might be the first in her family to have enrolled in college.

Is Ana aware of you, your concern for her? Sometimes you think *yes*. More often you think *No. Not at all.*

· · · · · · ·

I can't.

Or, *I don't think that I can...*

At the age of twenty-two, you were terrified at the prospect of teaching your first class.

English Composition. A large urban university. An evening class.

More than a quarter-century ago and yet—vivid in memory!

You had never taught before. You had a master's degree in English but had never been (like most of your graduate student friends, and your husband) a teaching assistant. Amazing to you now, that the chairman of an English Department in a quite reputable private university had hired you to teach though you'd had no experience teaching at all—had not once stood in front of a classroom. (He'd said afterward that he had been impressed by the written work of yours he'd seen, in national publications. He'd said that, in his experience, teaching was best picked up *on the fly*, like learning to ride a bicycle, or like sex.)

It had been thrilling to you, to be so selected over numerous others with experience, older than you. But it had not been so thrilling to contemplate the actual teaching. At twenty-two you would not be much older, in fact you would be younger, than many of your students enrolled in the university's night school division.

English composition! The most commonly taught of university courses, along with remedial English and math.

Your husband, young himself at the time, just thirty, had tried to dispel your terror. He'd tried to encourage you, tease you. Saying—*Don't be afraid, I can walk you into the classroom on my shoes.*

Such a silly notion, you'd laughed. Tears of apprehension in your eyes and yet you'd laughed, your husband had that power, to calm you.

Between your young husband and you, in those years. Much laughter.

You think you will live forever. Always it will be like this. You don't think—well, you don't think.

Your husband had a Ph.D. in English. He was an assistant professor at another, nearby university, he'd been a very successful teacher for several years. Gently he reasoned with you: what could possibly go wrong, once you'd prepared for the first class?

What could go wrong? Everything!

They won't pay attention to me. They will see that I am too young—inexperienced. They will laugh in derision. Some of them will walk out...

Your husband convinced you that such fears were groundless. Ridiculous. University students would not walk out of a class. Especially older students would not walk out of a class for which they'd paid tuition—it was a serious business to them, not a lark.

In this class, so long ago, were thirty students. Thirty! Overlarge for a composition class.

To you, thirty strangers. You broke into actual sweat, contemplating them. The prospect of entering the classroom was dazzling. A nightmare. For days beforehand you rehearsed your first words—*Hello! This is English one-oh-one and my name is*—which you hoped would not be stammered, and would be audible. For days you pondered—what should you *wear?*

On that crucial evening your husband drove you to the university. Your husband did not *walk you into the room on his shoes,* but he did accompany you to the assigned classroom in the ground floor of an old red-brick building. (Did your husband kiss you, for good luck? A brush of his lips on your cheek?) How breathless you were by this time, seeing your prospective students pass you oblivious of you.

Wish me luck.

I love you!

And so it happened when you stepped into the classroom, and took your place behind a podium in front of a blackboard, and introduced yourself to rows of strangers gazing at you with the most rapt interest you'd ever drawn from any strangers in your life—an unexpected and astonishing conviction flooded over you of *happiness.*

Knowing you were in the right place, at just the right time.

. . . .

You feel her absence keenly.

This day, a particularly wet, cold day Ana is absent from the workshop.

Reluctant to begin class you wait for several minutes. (For other students are arriving late.) Then, when it is evident that Ana will not be coming, you begin.

You have noticed that Ana sits in the same place at the table each week. She will arrive early, to assure this. Such (rigid?) behavior is the sign of a shy person; a person who has had enough upset in her life, and now wants a predictable routine; a person who chooses to rein in her emotions; a person who knows that, like internal hemorrhaging, emotions are not infinite, and can be fatal.

Tacitly the others have conceded Ana's place at the (farther) end of the table. No one would take Ana's chair, just as no one would take the Professor's usual seat.

Yet, no one mentions Ana's absence. So little impression has she made on the class, no one thinks to wonder aloud— *Hey, where is Ana?*

You ask for a volunteer, to provide Ana with the assignment for the following week. At first no one responds. Then a young woman raises her hand—*Sure! She's in my residence hall, I think.*

You might email or text Ana yourself. But you are thinking you would like someone from the workshop to volunteer, to forge a connection with Ana however slight.

That evening Ana sends you an email, apologizing for her absence. *Flu, infirmary, sorry to miss class. Will make up missing work.*

Ridiculous, you are *so relieved.*

Smiling, your heart suffused with—what? Hope like a helium-filled balloon.

When Ana returns to the workshop you tell her—*We missed you, Ana.*

True, to a degree. *You* missed her.

Naturally Ana has completed the assignment: the reading in the anthology, and the weekly prose piece. Though Ana is not one of the more imaginative writers, Ana is the most diligent of students.

Hers has been good work, acceptable work so far this semester. It is careful work, precisely written English, surprisingly free of errors for one whose speech is uncertain. Is this the utterance of clenched jaws?—you wonder. Maybe Ana would like to scream.

You will encourage her to write more freely. From the heart.

You will tell her—in fact, you will tell the class—*Write what feels like life to you. It need not be "true"—your writing will make it "true."*

Ana frowns distractedly, staring down at the table. She knows that you are (obliquely) criticizing her work, which the others have discussed politely, without much to say about it. For all her pose of indifference Ana is highly sensitive.

You have encouraged your students to write, not memoir, but *memoir-like* fiction. You do not (truly!) want these young people to open their veins and pour out their life's blood for the diversion of others but neither do you want them to attempt arch, artificial fiction derivative of work by the most-read fiction writers of the era—for that they cannot do, and certainly they cannot do well.

Others in the class take up the challenge, excited. *Write what feels like life to you.*

Ana takes back her prose piece from you. Ana's eyes slide away from yours and will not engage.

You had written—*Promising! But something that anyone might have written. What does "Ana" have to say?*

Away from the seminar room that is the *happy place,* you ponder your obsession with this student. For the first time acknowledging the word—*obsession.*

Telling yourself that now you've made the acknowledgment, the *obsession* will begin to fade.

· · · · · · ·

And then, in the seventh week of the semester, long past the time when you'd have thought that any undergraduate could surprise you, Ana hands in something very different from the cautious prose she has been writing.

The assignment is a dramatic monologue. Just a page or two. In the "memoirist" mode.

Here is urgent, intense work by Ana. Not cautious at all—a bold plunge into stream-of-consciousness speech uttered (seemingly) by an adolescent daughter of (Guatemalan?) (illegal?) immigrants stranded in a nightmare detention center at the Texas border in Laredo.

The other young writers take notice. It is requested that Ana read the monologue aloud.

Oh, I—I can't...

Stammering *no,* blushing fiercely but the others insist.

From a prose poem of Ana's:

I thought the eucalyptus had burst into flame, I'd seen it and ran away screaming. And then—years later they laugh at me and told me no, that had not happened to me but to my little sister.

And when I remember my brother beaten by our father with his fists they tell me no, not just my brother but me, as well. But they are not laughing.

In the foster home there are three girls named Mya.

Those acts perpetrated upon one of the Myas are perpetrated upon the others.

We do not know your name but your face will always be known to us.

Astonishing and wonderful—Ana is writing with such passion now.

Less guardedly, and less circumspectly. Wonderful too, how others in the seminar take up her work with excitement and admiration.

This is not conventional "fiction"—there are few "characters"—minimal "description"—"settings." All is dreamlike, rapid-fire.

In fragments it is revealed that a girl named "Mya" has lived in one or more foster homes in the Southwest. Albuquerque, Tucson. In the home are (illegal?) Central American immigrants. There are bribes to be paid. There are hopes for visas, green cards. There are knives, guns. Brutal beatings when debts are not repaid. Shootings, woundings, blood-soaked mattresses. A ghastly scene in an emergency room where an eighteen-year-old Guatemalan hemorrhages to death, and a laconic scene in a morgue in which a drug-addled woman attempts to identify an estranged and badly mutilated husband. Hiding from law enforcement officers, rummaging dumpsters for food. Shoplifting. Unexpected cruelty in the foster home, and unexpected kindness.

Homeless children, adolescents. A girl seeking out a younger sister who has been sent to live in a foster home.

There was no choice. My mother believed our father would kill her if she did not leave.

...first there were three Myas in the foster home. Then there were two Myas. Then there was one Mya.

Then, none.

You are filled with dread, you have gone too far. Your shy, unassertive student has begun writing *what feels like life*—she has thrown off restraint.

It is true, you have triumphed—as a writing instructor. But this is a precarious triumph—(maybe). As if you have prized open a shell, the pulsing life of the defenseless mollusk within is exposed.

One of the most imaginative writers in the class, whose name is Philip, whose major is astrophysics and whose favored writers are Borges, Calvino, Cortázar, declares that Ana's prose poetry is *beautiful and terrible as a Möbius strip.*

Ana is deeply moved to hear these words. You have seen how Philip has been casting sidelong glances at Ana, over the weeks; now Ana lifts her eyes to his face.

Much attention is paid in the workshop to Ana's prose. Her sentences, paragraphs—headlong plunges of language. There is praise for Ana's spare, elliptical dialogue which is buried in the text as if it might be interior and not uttered aloud at all.

No one cares to address Ana's powerful subject matter. Desperate persons, domestic violence, a hint of sexual assault. *Three girls named Mya in the foster home.*

Amid their admiration the others are uneasy. It is considered bad manners—the violation of an implicit taboo—to ask if anyone's work is based upon her experiences, at least when the work is so extreme. And you have taken care to instruct the students, memoirist writing is *not memoir.* Even memoir is not "autobiography" but understood to be more poetic and impressionistic, less literal and complete.

At the end of the discussion Ana is flushed with pleasure. Unless it's an excited sort of dread. Never have you seen Ana so intense, so involved in the workshop.

You would not dare reach out to touch her wrist now, her burning-hot skin would scald your fingers.

The following Thursday Ana is not in the seminar room when you arrive.

Everyone waits for Ana's arrival. The chair in which she usually sits is left unoccupied. But she does not appear.

Your heart is seized with dismay. You are sure it's as you'd feared—Ana regrets what she revealed to the class, she regrets being led to such openness.

Having written what she has written, that cannot now be retracted.

I am so sorry, Ana. Forgive me.

You don't write such an email. Never!

From your husband you learned never to impose your emotions upon students. Never to assume to know what they are thinking and feeling, that is (but) what you imagine they are thinking and feeling, unless they tell you; and it would be rare indeed for them to tell you.

You are the adult. You are the professional. You must prevail.

And then: by chance you encounter Ana in a store near the university.

Indeed it is but *by chance.* Indeed *you have not been following Ana.*

Seeing too, another time—how alone Ana appears. How small, vulnerable.

Inside an oversized winter coat falling nearly to her ankles, that looks like a hand-me-down.

Her face is flushed from the cold, her eyes startled and damp. Faint shadows like bruises in her perfect skin, beneath her eyes.

Though you can see that Ana would (probably) prefer not to say hello it is not possible for you to avoid each other. You greet Ana with a friendly smile as you would any student, ignoring her nervousness; she stammers *Hello, Professor...*

Ana is embarrassed, awkward. Still, Ana manages to smile at her professor.

Telling you apologetically that she'd meant to write to you, to explain why she'd had to miss another class: there'd been a family emergency, she'd had to spend time on the phone with several relatives. Ana speaks so rapidly, in faltering English, you halfway wonder if she is telling the truth. Yet in her face an expression of such genuine dismay you are sure that she must be telling some part of the truth.

You are thinking *If this were a story...*you would invite Ana to have coffee with you, perhaps you would walk together in the lightly falling snow, and talk. Ana would confide in you at last, directly; as, it has seemed to you, she is confiding in you indirectly, in her writing. Ana would reveal herself the survivor of abuse, a broken and devastated household. A traumatized child in need of advice, protection...

But that does not happen. Will not happen. For this is not a story, and not a fiction. This is actual life, that does not bend easily to your fantasies.

The moment passes. You move on. You do not glance after Ana, as, you are sure, Ana does not glance after you.

It is true, you are desperately lonely. But you understand that yours is an adult loneliness that no adolescent stranger can assuage.

· · · · · · ·

Recalling your shock, and subsequently melancholy, when the first class of your life came to an end.

How you'd actually wept... *I will never have such wonderful students again.*

Your husband comforted you though (surely) he'd been amused.

Twenty-seven years ago.

· · · · · · ·

As abruptly as it seemed to have begun, the semester has ended.

The final workshop in the wood-paneled seminar room at the top of the smooth-worn staircase in North Hall.

And then, reading week—between the end of classes and the start of exams. You will see students through this week, you have made appointments with each of the writers in the workshop. Following these conferences it's likely that you will not see most of the students again.

After such intimacy, abrupt detachment. The way of teaching—semester following semester.

Professor! Hello...

There is Ana, in the doorway of your office. Accompanied by two tensely smiling adults—parents?

You don't expect this. You are totally surprised. You'd thought—what had you thought?

A lost girl, an abused girl. An orphan.

Though Ana appears to be virtually quivering with nerves, or with excitement, she has brought her parents to meet you—*Elena and Carlos Fallas.* Ana's pride in the situation, her thrilled face, shining eyes, the way she clasps her parents' hands in hers, urging them to enter your office—it is very touching, you are moved nearly to tears.

Ana's parents are so *young.* Especially the mother who is Ana's height, small-boned, with beautiful dark eyes. Haltingly the parents speak to you in heavily accented English. They are visiting from San Diego, they say. They have heard much about *you.*

Through a roaring in your ears you hear Ana speaking of her favorite class, her writing class, how you helped her to write *as if your life depended upon it.*

How you'd told her—*It need not be true, your writing will make it true.*

Ana is breathless, daring. What an achievement it has been for your shyest student to have brought her parents to meet you! How long has Ana been practicing these words, this encounter...

The scene seems impossible to you. Unreal. How had you so misread Ana Fallas? Her seeming lack of interest in the seminar, and in you ... Her sorrowful expression, her isolation ...

Had you misinterpreted, and Ana is not telling the fullest truth now? But rather, performing for her parents? And for you?

The melancholy was not feigned, you are sure. The sorrow in her eyes. Yet—here is a very different Ana, laughing as she discreetly corrects her parents' English, vivacious and sparkling, happy.

Ana has plaited her hair into a sleekly black braid. She has painted her fingernails coral. She is wearing, not baggy clothes, but attractive bright-colored clothing that is a perfect size for her small body. The little gold cross glitters around her neck. Ana is very pretty, and she is adored by her parents. She is not an abused child, she is certainly not an orphan.

Astonishingly, you hear—*My favorite professor.*

You are determined not to betray this astonishment. You are determined to speak despite the roaring in your ears. Assuring Ana's eager parents that Ana has been an excellent student. A very promising writer. Like few young writers, Ana can learn from criticism—constructive criticism. Ana's imagination is fertile, seemingly boundless. You are giddy as a drunkard. Words tumble from your mouth, you are shameless. You will say anything to please these people, you want only to make them happy, to make them less ill-at-ease in your professorial presence.

You will not confess—*I have been so mistaken about your daughter. I am ashamed...*

She is not the person I had imagined. You are not the people. Forgive me!

Ana's parents have brought you a beautifully wrapped little gift. Your heart sinks, you hope it isn't expensive. (That size? Could be a small clock. A watch.) You have not the heart to decline their generosity, but it is considered a breach of academic ethics, at least at this university, to accept gifts from the parents of students, even small gifts.

The card from Ana you will accept, with thanks. The gift you will pass to the departmental secretary.

Ana's parents are less nervous now. They tell you how proud they are of their daughter, the first in the family to attend a four-year college. How grateful for the scholarship that brought her here—though it is so far from home. How honored to meet you.

When they leave you stand in the doorway of your office staring after them, still disbelieving, dazed. *So mistaken. How possible...*

The little gift you leave on your desk for the time being. The card from Ana you open: *Thank you, Professor, for giving me the key to my life.*

And then, returning home later that evening.

A mild shock—the door is unlocked.

Turn the knob, and the door opens. Not for the first time since your husband has died. It is a careless habit, away for hours and the house unlocked and darkened.

You have become careless with your life. Indifferent.

Entering an empty house from which all meaning has fled.

Once, this was a *happy place*. That seems like a bad joke now.

Each room in this house is a kind of exile. You avoid most of the rooms, you keep in motion. Difficult to find a place to sit, a place where you are comfortable sitting. Almost at once you feel restless, anxious. Your fingers clutch at the hollow in your throat, you have difficulty breathing.

He has been gone how many months. Still you cannot— quite—acknowledge the word *dead*.

Once, you'd known precisely how many weeks, days. Down to the hour.

But the house is still as deserted. This place from which happiness has drained like water seeping into earth.

You have tried to explain to your husband, as you try to explain to him so many things, for he is patient, unjudging— how you were mistaken about Ana, for so long. The stubbornness in your misperception, the *hurt*. You have tried, and failed, to explain to him why Ana has meant so much to you. And why it has all ended, as it has ended.

It is frightening to you, in this empty and darkened house— *What else has eluded you, that is staring you in the face? About what else have you been mistaken?*

The Department of No Solution

YIYUN LI

A FEW YEARS AGO I was summoned to the local office of Homeland Security for fingerprinting, but my fingers did not yield acceptable results. The staff wiped the screen violently and then examined my fingers, and the routine procedure was prolonged without any promising prospect. For the next few months, I received a notice every other week, summoning me for another fingerprint, until, after the sixth failure, a final notice instructed me never to show up again but wait for the police department to contact me.

Who wants to deal with an incomplete product repeatedly? In retrospect this could make a good story, but even a good story might become a wrong story the moment it's told. A woman at a party, upon hearing my fingerprinting misadventure, said what a great metaphor my fingers were. You're a fiction writer, she said; and you've typed away your identity. Metaphor? No immigrant lives for a metaphor. Were I a housekeeper, my fingerprints, eroded by cleaning detergent, might not register better.

I told the story one more time after that, to a worse response. Two young women called the story Kafkaesque. I had no use for Kafka. Besides, Kafkaesque is becoming a shortcut when people have fewer fresh words to say. After that I stopped telling the story.

How's life? a friend asked the other day.
Oh, life, I said. The department of no solution.

Exactly, she said. The good thing is, you can file away a lot. Everything between Chekhov and Kafka goes in that department.

What would I have left? I wondered.

A crew of movers came to pack up our house, and at the end of the day one of them asked if he could have my copy of *The Death of Ivan Ilyich*. An odd request, I thought, but why not?

The next day they moved us into a new house. In the middle of the night, I got a text from the lead mover—not the one who had asked for the book. Ma'am, the text said, I have a side business of meeting women discreetly for sex. Any time, just text me an hour ahead of time, and I can meet you at a hotel or anywhere.

I could have felt indignant or disgusted or horrified. But I laughed. It was the first night we were in the new house. We had put down the deposit for it on the same day my son died, in that order, so you could say we put down the deposit for a nonexistent future. He had fallen in love with the house, and after he died we made the decision to proceed with the purchase.

I told a friend about the mover's text. Does moving houses for people offer an opportunity for him to scout clients? she said. She could have felt indignant or disgusted or horrified, but she too laughed. That autumn there was not much to laugh about, nor in the seasons after.

How have you been? asked the psychiatrist when I sat down in her office. I had only met her once, the week before my son's death.

Not so well, I said, and updated her on the news.

She clicked her tongue and said how horrible it was, and then looked at my chart. Thank God you have another son, she said.

I thought, I thank God for nothing.

Later she said, it's time to think if you want another child.

Oh no, I don't think so, I said.

I'm not asking you to make the decision now, she said. She looked at the chart again. You still have some time, but not a lot.

I thought of telling her that in the old days women my age might be grandmothers. But perhaps in the old days losing a child was more of a common fate for parents. My grandparents lost one. A friend remembered his little sister's death. Another friend told me about her little brother's death. The list could go on.

I hope you're not going back to her, a friend said after I told her about the visit to the psychiatrist. As a matter of fact, I said, I'll probably still go to her. A dear friend once said that we can always laugh when someone says things that are so horrible and so wrong, and when we laugh the horrible wrong things cannot touch us. The worst are those well-intentioned, mediocre and sensible words, she said. We cannot protect ourselves against their sensibleness.

I took a week off after my son died and then went back to work. In the first class I taught, in that zone of after, a student turned in a story that haphazardly left a woman dead. Neither her parents nor her sibling seemed to feel anything about the death, and two pages later she was entirely forgotten. In the discussion another student said, I don't think a story should just let a death happen to a character without leaving anyone to feel anything.

The author of the story defended herself: but I wanted to write something fluffy so we can laugh at the characters.

I stared at her. Not everyone, I thought, deserves to be metamorphosed by Kafka, but perhaps everyone has a place in a Chekhov story.

The friend who told me to put everything between Kafka and Chekhov into the department of no solution: one day she came to work and said her daughter's best friend had committed suicide. Fifteen, a year younger than my son.

I saw her the other day and said, how are the girl's parents?

How are they? she said. How are you?

I know, I said. The worst question, isn't it?

Still, we ask all the time. How are you? How are you doing? How are you feeling?

We don't say: How are you handling the department of no solution? How much have you filed away? How much do you have left in your life?

A few months after my son died, I had a conversation with the mother of one of his childhood friends. She told me that she had learned, from another parent, that my son had texted a couple friends to say farewell before he died, but he had not texted her daughter. She went home and told the girl about the messages that others had received and she had not.

The texts he had sent to his friends were news to me. To be brought back to that moment of fatality was worse than when the policemen asked me to sit down and said, there's no better way to say this, ma'am.

The woman said of her daughter, she feels sad that she didn't get a text. Why did he text the others but not her? I can see it'll take her a long time to process that.

Oh shut up, I thought. Shut up shut up shut up. Instead, I said, oh, but you must trust that he always thought of her as a special friend.

(My friend was wrong that when people said the most horrible things, the most wrong things, we could always laugh. Sooner or later we would run out of laughter.)

I don't think he ever thought of her as a confidante, the woman said of my son and her daughter. She always thought of him as her best friend. It'll take her a long time to recover.

No one, I wanted to say to the woman, is special enough for another person. Ask Chekhov. Ask Kafka. Ask my dead son.

I said nothing, though. One day, I thought, one day in a near or a distant future, when the conversation between her and me was filed away in the department of no solution, it would become less of a horror story.

Ithaca

MARY NORRIS

THE GIG WAS AT THE SACRED ROOT KAVA BAR AND TEA
LOUNGE, in Ithaca, New York. My sister, Baby Dee—a musician—had put together a tour with our nephew Blake, also
a musician. They had rehearsed together via Skype, Dee on
accordion in the Netherlands teaching her songs to Blake on
guitar in Oregon. I had volunteered my services as driver. I'd
been to several of Dee's shows—in Barcelona, Madrid, Amster-
dam, Cleveland—but as a fan, not as a roadie. We lingered over
brunch in Hudson on a mild Saturday morning in February.
"Never be in a hurry to leave someplace nice," Dee said. Eventually, we packed the Mini for the drive upstate: Blake wedged
into the back seat with the guitar case and the squeezebox, Dee
sitting tall in the passenger seat, her hair, in a frizzy red top-
knot, brushing the moon roof. The merch—CDs and vinyl—
was in the trunk with the rest of the luggage.

We drove to Ithaca along back roads in pouring rain. As
I slid in the first disk of the *Odyssey*, in the Robert Fitzgerald
translation, I felt the car hydroplane. Briefly, we were afloat.
I had forgotten that the first four books of the *Odyssey* are all
about Telemachus. Blake was on his cell phone, lining up acts
for a music festival he was producing—where did this well-
formed young man with the dark blond dreadlocks get the
impresario gene?—but Dee listened with me. By the time we
pulled into town, Telemachus had left Ithaca and arrived in
Sparta to consult Menelaus. Helen takes one look at him and

says, "This must be Odysseus's son." After they talk, she drugs him with nepenthe so that he will forget his troubles and get a good night's sleep.

Meanwhile, in this other Ithaca, it was dark, and still raining, and we couldn't find the venue. The address we had been given didn't match any house on the street. Finally, someone at a strip-mall pizzeria directed us to a three-story red brick building on a corner lot with a huge sign that said Cornell Daily Sun. A plaque for the Community Labyrinth should have tipped me off that this was the place. A side door that looked as if it led to a boiler room had a mandala painted on it and swirly lettering that read Sacred Root Kava Bar.

Down a broad set of stairs, in a big room, smoky with incense, was a square island of a bar. It looked like an ordinary bar, and had an ordinary bartender behind it, except that it was set in a different, nonalcoholic dimension. There was a guy on his laptop and a woman with her hair in a heavy braid and two boys playing backgammon. We were looking for someone named Bubba, but the bartender said that Bubba was not there. The sound guy showed up. As the headliner, Dee was last on the program, and her needs were simple—a single microphone—so she was last in the sound check. While we waited, Dee said, "Let's have a kava."

The bartender explained that kava was a root, and it made you calm and serene. Not everyone likes the taste, though, so it was mixed with either chocolate almond milk or vanilla coconut milk. We shared a bowl of the chocolate almond, ladling the kava into coconut shells, which rested on pedestals made of upright shank bones—the kind used for ossobuco. Our first taste of the sacred root required a ritual, the bartender said: clap your hands twice, throw your arms in the air, and shout, "Boo *hah!*" Everyone at the bar joined in: "Boo *hah!*" The kava was cold—I had expected it to be warm—and tasted like chalk. "I forgot to tell you," the bartender said. "You might experience some numbness of the tongue."

The kava bar had a cozy, well-lit gift shop, stocked with incense and tchotchkes, but when I asked where to set up Dee's merchandise—part of my job as a roadie—I was directed to a dark table along the wall, where I was unlikely to attract attention. But I didn't complain. Dee had said once, in Madrid, after suffering through a drive from Barcelona during which two members of the entourage had argued relentlessly about Islam, "One negative word can do a lot of damage." I would not be the one to utter words of ill omen. There was no dressing room, but the owner said that Dee could use the kitchen. When I went in there later, Dee had set up an altar: a picture of her teacher, a Tibetan Buddhist monk, surrounded by shallow bowls filled with water. Over her clothes, she was wearing a nightgown—white, with sprigs of violets—which doubled as a makeup smock. Blake had changed shirts and was tuning his guitar. He is a quiet kid, not in a tense way, but mellow and companionable. At the utility sink, the owner mixed a batch of kava in a five-gallon bucket and recited for me the names of the Finger Lakes—Genesee, Cayuga, Seneca, Skaneateles, pronounced Skinny Atlas, not Skin Needle Ease. He had come from California to make a go of this kava bar in Ithaca.

My associations with Ithaca were few, all with people who had studied or taught at Cornell: a beloved shrink, a veterinarian, Vladimir Nabokov. I couldn't picture any of them cradling a kava—well, maybe the vet, who kept her hair and nails long, perhaps the better to relate to cats and dogs? People began trickling in, guys dressed in flannel shirts and stocking caps—the uniform of craft brewers everywhere—women in boots and prairie skirts. A friend of Dee's, Sarah, a trans woman who had moved to Ithaca from Austin, Texas, was playing drums with her own group. She had agreed to let us sleep at her house. For one act, the performers had set up a wall of box fans, wired to light up during the music. I took a break, climbing the broad stairs to the rainy street to buy beer and stash it in the car. We were going to need it later.

Baby Dee wore a filmy low-cut gray-mauve outfit that she'd put together from lingerie—slips and petticoats—bought at the Goodwill and dyed. On a hanger it looked like a collection of rags, but onstage it was gossamer, ethereal, like the wings of a moth. More people had come in during the break, and they stopped milling around and sat on the floor to listen. Dee perched on a stool with her accordion; Blake watched Dee's hands and listened and added sonic filigree on guitar—he got better, bolder, with every show. The set included songs Dee wrote twenty years ago, when she came back to Cleveland to take care of our parents—something it had certainly never occurred to me to do. I still can't listen to those songs without a lump in my throat. There's one about Dee's fear, as a child, of being late for dinner—"He's going to kill me when I get home." People take it literally: they think Dad was a child abuser, whereas really he was only strict about dinnertime. A song called "So Bad" has the lyric "Jesus got my mom in there, and beat her up so bad." Listeners think it's about all kinds of things: Muslims, religious intolerance, Dad (again). I alone in the crowd, apart from Dee, knew its origins: Our mother had taken us with her to church when she went to confession, and because the confessional boxes were all occupied—it must have been Lent—a priest led her into the sacristy to hear her confession face to face. Left in the pew with me, my little brother (as Dee was then) wept inconsolably.

It was appropriate that Dee was working the family theme on this tour: with Blake along and me at the wheel, it was a family act. Dee, who was once a church organist, has also written bawdy songs, and for these she turns to the piano, which always reminds me of our grandmother at the upright. (In olden times, Grandma had played piano for silent movies.) One of Dee's so-called stupid songs is called "Big Titty Bee Girls (From Dino Town)," and there's a "hymn," a rollicking sing-along called "The Song of Self-Acceptance," inspired by our mother, who crowed one night, "I'm not the only pisspot in the house." I love these numbers—I always request them. Dee says it's easy to go from the dirges, as she calls the quiet, heartbreaking songs, to the stupid songs, but once you've broken the spell it's almost impossible to get back.

Afterward, Dee took over the merch table and did a brisk business. A woman named Mara introduced herself to me and said, "You're staying at my house." Mara was married to Sarah. It had stopped raining by the time we left, and the night had turned frosty. We followed the women's car, zigzagging through the streets of Ithaca, and turned into the driveway of a modest house with a patch of lawn out front. Inside, when Sarah opened a door, two dogs burst out and tore around the house. The women both had good jobs, one with the university and the other with an art gallery, and their home was full of collectibles. The coffee table was an old bellows from a blacksmith shop, with a potted plant sunk in a round hole. A wall at the back of the house was hung with vintage thermometers. Sarah and Mara were newlyweds; their marriage license was posted on the refrigerator door. They sat close together on the couch and told stories about Sarah's father as we shared the beer.

The women prepared beds for us, as Helen did for Telemachus in Sparta. A sofa bed was made up for Blake in the living room. Sarah showed Dee to a room behind the kitchen. Mara took me upstairs to a bedroom with a vintage quilt and a space heater and a window overlooking the street. We rested comfortably that night in Ithaca, which, though not an island, felt remote and separate—the home of girls who do what they please.

We woke to a sifting of snow on the grass, and instead of eating pancakes at the local diner, as planned, Dee said we should probably get on the road. The women were gracious. A good host does not delay a guest who feels the need to move on. I brushed the snow off the Mini—my duty as the roadie—and we crammed ourselves in again. The snow was not so heavy that it impaired driving, but the tiny holes for the win-

dow washer fluid had frozen over. At a stoplight, I looked for
something pointy—an earring wire, a sharpened pencil—to
poke through the ice. Sarah had given Dee a CD that came
packaged, domestically, with a threaded needle: perfect. The
snow laid a beautiful light covering over the fields and trees
along the country roads.

"What ever happened to Bubba?" I asked, once we were
under way.

"Yeah," Blake said from the back seat. "I was wondering
about that, too."

"I heard he was sick or something," Dee said, shrugging.
"Anyway, that turned out to be a good show. You never can
tell."

Next stop: Providence.

Camp Artemis

CASTLE FREEMAN, JR.

How is it that, these days, things are happening a hundred years ago that never happened a hundred years ago before? Suddenly, the centennials accumulate: Teddy Roosevelt, Wilson, and Taft; General Pershing and Pancho Villa; Arizona and New Mexico; the Income Tax. And, finally, the First World War, the Great War, the War to End War that, we now know, didn't quite do the trick, but did sweep up two million American boys into the adventure of their lives—and, for above a hundred thousand of them, their deaths.

One American boy in particular I'm thinking of, a mysterious figure, hardly seen, whose full name I never knew and who must be gone for, by now, forty or fifty years.

In the summer I turned twenty-three, I was quartered in a defunct girls' camp beside a tiny green pond livid with algae; a dilapidated facility having no campers, no equipment, and no amenities apart from blue, distant views of Mount Monadnock. The place was called Camp Artemis, and its four bunkhouses, knocked together years earlier out of rough two-by-fours, tar paper, asphalt shingles, and mosquito screen, were, like its name, of Classical inspiration, styled, as they were, Minerva, Juno, Ceres, Athena.

Camp Artemis belonged to my gentle, Unitarian Aunt Grace and Uncle Ted, but they had shuttered the place and put it up for sale. The summer I'm telling of, they were traveling in Nepal. Our arrangement was that I got room and board at the camp, and in return I held myself in readiness for the real estate agents in Brattleboro to show the place to prospects—prospects who numbered zero. I also did what I could to repair broken windows and leaking roofs, and I looked around for better, more permanent employment, not easy to find in post-agricultural, post-industrial, post-capitalist, post-socialist, post-modern Vermont.

I say employment wasn't easy to find, but in fact it wasn't only the finding that was difficult, it was, even more, the keeping. As a new hire, it seemed, I had bad luck. By September, I felt as though I'd had as many jobs die under me as Colonel Custer had had cavalry mounts.

Newly arrived in the state, I thought I would get on the road crew in my town, but I soon found out the road crew was a closed corporation, like a guild, almost a family affair—somebody else's family, not mine.

"What would you do for me?" the road foreman asked.

"I don't know," I said. "What do you need? Potholes. I could fill potholes."

"If you're filling potholes, what do I do with Steve and Kenny?"

"Something else, then."

"You ever run a grader?"

"It's been awhile."

"I didn't think so. Can you drive truck?"

"Sure."

"No, I don't mean drive *a* truck. I mean drive truck. A big truck."

"I could learn."

"Probably you could. But, then, if you did, what about Bill? What's he do?"

"I'd be a trainee," I said.

"That's all I got, is trainees," said the foreman. He shook his head. "I don't see this working," he said. "Unless you were ready to come on for no pay. Then, maybe, I could help you."

"Then *you* could help *me*?"

"Maybe, if you'll work for free. What about it?"

"Thanks for your time," I said.

Presently, I was hired as porter to a country auctioneer. I carried sale lots onto the stage, held them up, and turned them this way and that so the buyers could get a good look while Dale, the auctioneer, called the bidding. Rocking chairs, canoes, guitars, saxophones, beds, butter churns, oil portraits, firearms, bicycles, every kind of hand tool—I schlepped and showed them all. I enjoyed my job. It was like working in somebody's attic, or in an endlessly self-regenerating museum. I was content, until the auctioneer's son was let out of Juvenile Hall. He needed a job. He got one. He got mine. I got a warm handclasp, a crisp fifty-dollar bill, and the road.

Worked for a print shop in Brattleboro—proofreader. This was an old-fashioned hot-metal shop, a doomed triceratops among the ascendant digital mammalians. The shop floor was a clacking, clattering chaos of lofty iron Mergenthaler machines, the proof department, a bathroom-sized cell where four of us sat like monks before tilted desks, chain-smoking Luckies as we attended to the galleys, AAs, and page proofs of our betters, including (that I recall) Samuel Eliot Morison, Danielle Steel, and John le Carré. The concern went under shortly after I joined up, and I well remember the last day, when the laid-off, paid-off, pissed-off compositors dismantled the linotype machines and the type foundries and tossed them out the windows into the parking lot to be broken up for scrap metal by other compositors swinging sledgehammers.

Pumped gas at a station on Route 9—same place that's the vet hospital today. I reckoned I was bulletproof at last. Not the most absorbing work, perhaps; humble work, but safe and sound and, surely, immune to failure. Not so. My engagement was brief (though memorable). I had the three-to-eleven shift. In my second week on the job, one busy Friday evening, I had people in a hurry at all three pumps. I was running hard and forgot to turn off the pump and remove the hose from the filling port of somebody's truck. The truck drove off. The hose and nozzle were ripped violently from the pump stand and dragged over the concrete behind the departing truck. There was a spark, and Number Two Pump went up with a roar like all the horns in hell and a fireball that was a pretty good fireball, everybody said.

The next morning, Carlton, the owner, had me into his office.

"I'm not sure you're cut out for this work," he told me.

"By 'this work,' you mean pumping gas?"

"That's right."

"I wouldn't have thought anybody was or wasn't cut out for pumping gas," I said.

"I wouldn't have, either," Carlton said. "But it looks like we were both wrong. Doesn't it?" He nodded toward the window and the apron beyond it, where the reeking, ruined skeleton of Number Two jutted into the sky, black and stark as a gallows.

By now it was nearly Labor Day. School would be opening. I thought I'd try for a teaching position. Having no experience or training whatever as a teacher, I didn't think I had much of a shot at the public system, but that left private schools, which, I hoped, might be desperate to fill positions for the year that would start in a week or so.

I had my eye on an institution I felt was a likely candidate, in the shape of the Putney School, a small boarding school not far from me that was founded and run on the so-called Progressive principles of John Dewey and his followers. At Putney, I reckoned, I had a kind of hereditary advantage. The school I had gone to, in another part of the country, had been started and led by Dewey himself. I knew the form then, had imbibed it from early childhood. I had other qualifications, as well. If I had no experience in teaching, I had plenty in being taught; indeed, being a student was all I had ever done. I also had an honorable discharge from a famous university. I even had an old tweed jacket. I would become a Friend, Guide, and Companion to Youth, a Schoolmaster.

Putney thought not. I arrived at the school having scheduled a job interview in a phone call to the chairman of the English Department. Now I learned that he was home sick; I would be meeting with the head of school, herself. So much the better, I thought. I was shown into her office.

The head of school proved to be an Englishwoman in her sixties, thin as a rake, with an aristocratic accent and an appraising gaze, a patient gaze, not unfriendly, but skeptical. She sat me at one end of the leather couch in her office and took the other.

"Where will you start?" she asked me.

This was an agreeable surprise. Did I already have the job? It looked like the business was going to be easier than I had expected. That would be a welcome change from recent history, wouldn't it?

"Am I hired?" I asked the head.

"Of course you are. I thought you and George had all that sorted."

George was the ailing English teacher. I thought it best to be vague.

"Ah, yes," I said.

"Where will you start?" the head asked me again.

"Ah, well, ah. *Beowulf?*"

"I beg your pardon?"

"You're right," I said. "Boring. Disappointing. Gloomy. Quite unsuitable. What about Chaucer?"

"What about him?"

"Well," I said. "You asked where I'd start. At the beginning, I thought, yes? Start at the bottom?"

"But, see here," said the head of school. "George told us always to start at the top. So as not to have dribbles."

"Dribbles?"

The head of school nodded. "Dribbles," she said. "I mean to

say, to avoid dribbles. As you proceed. You proceed up-to-down. You proceed top-to-bottom. Covering any dribbles. George was very particular about that."

"George?"

"Head of plant maintenance."

"Plant maintenance?"

The head fixed me with an odd look. "Hang on," she said. "Whom did you speak to?"

"George," I said.

"George what?"

"George Tugwell."

"Oh, dear," said the head of school. "Now I grasp it. *That* George is chairman of English. George *Palmer* is in charge of plant maintenance. Why do you suppose you're here?"

"To teach English."

"Well, there you have it," said the head. "I thought you'd come to paint the library."

"Then there's no job in the English Department?"

"I'm afraid not."

"But George—George Tugwell—said we should meet. He said we should talk."

"Yes," said the head of school. "George will talk to anybody, bless him. Won't he? I don't know where we'd be without George."

· · · · · · ·

It was that same afternoon, on my beaten and disconsolate retreat from Putney, that I noticed a hitchhiker standing alongside Route 5. In those days, half the hippies, pilgrims, prophets, idealists, revolutionaries, and delinquents between Philadelphia and Portland were to be found on the roads of Vermont with their thumbs out; but this wayfarer was not one of them. He was no kid: an aged figure, bent, grizzled, and gimpy, leaning heavily on a stick. I pulled up and threw open the passenger's door, and the old party climbed in, then reached awkwardly across himself with his left hand to close the door. When he did, I saw he was missing most of his right forearm.

With an effortful heave, he shut the door and sat back in his seat. "Thankth," he said. "I'm in." Then he pulled his seatbelt partway out and held it, but didn't buckle it.

"No belt?" I asked him.

"Don't like them," the hitchhiker said. "Don't trust them. I'll just hold it tho it don't thquawk at uth." The old fellow appeared to have about a half-dozen teeth, and he whistled a little when he spoke.

I got us back on the road, southbound. "Where are you going?" I asked my passenger. "Brattleboro?"

"On over the line," he said. "Bernardston. Get my ticket."

"Your ticket?"

"Math Lottery," my passenger said. "I get my ticket, every time. You know the little crossroads thtore, there?"

"You can show me," I said.

"You ain't going to Bernardston, though. Nobody ith."

"I'll take you," I said. "Glad to. I don't have anything else to do. Maybe I'll get a ticket for myself."

"You'd better. Payout's fifty million, this time. Not bad for a buck a ticket."

"We'll split it," I said.

"Goddamn right, we will," said the old gent. "You at that thchool, are you?" He tilted his head back the way we had come from, toward Putney.

"It doesn't look like it," I said.

"You a teacher?"

"The school didn't think so."

"You look like a teacher."

"That's what I thought," I said.

"They missed the goddamned boat, all right: thmart kid like you, wants to work, looks right, talks right. And they brush him off. Shit."

I looked at my rider. I'd become aware of a faint smell of alcohol about him. Maybe not so faint. Now he reached into his pants pocket and came out with a dented tin flask. He unscrewed the cap and took a quick nip. Then he wiped the flask's neck on his sleeve and offered it to me. I shook my head.

"Go ahead," he said.

"What is it?"

"Don't know. Thomething." He sniffed the flask. "Cherry Bounce? Apricot? Can't tell. Thmeller's thot. Go on, have a little bootht."

"No, thanks," I said.

"Not a drinker?"

"Well, not too much, I guess."

"Thmart fella. Like I thaid." He screwed the cap back on his flask and held it under his damaged right arm.

"Thath a good thchool, back there," said my rider. "Rich kidth. One of the Kennedy kidth goeth there. Might be more than one."

We were back to Putney, it looked like, a painful subject. "How did you injure your arm?" I asked.

"I didn't injure it. Thomebody elth did."

"Who?"

"Who? I don't know: thome boche."

"You mean a German?"

"A boche, and a thon of a boche. I never thaw him. Woke up in the drething thtation. Down to an arm and a half. Must have been a thell. Medic thaid it wath cut that clean, a thurgeon might have done it. He thought that wath funny. Fuck him. Wathn't hith arm."

"You were in the war?"

"First war," he said. "The thuckerth' war."

"Suckers'?"

"Sure. Look: troop thip left New York on November Thirty, nineteen-seventeen, got back June Two, nineteen-nineteen. Five hundred and theventy-theven days in Franth. Got home and found out now you couldn't buy a drink in the U-Eth-A. Thucker'th war, up and down. Not but what they all ain't."

"Not all of them," I reminded him. "What about World War Two?"

"Thame pig, different dreth. They're all alike, thon, warth. Rich man'th war, poor man'th fight. You know?"

I had fallen in with a species of Green Mountain Bolshevik, it seemed. "What do you do?" I asked him.

"I'm retired. Waiting for my ticket to turn up. You?"

"I'm looking for work."

"What kind of work?"

"Anything, really. I've been looking for some time. Weeks. I'll try anything."

"Is that right? Well, then, I'm thinking you mutht be the kid blew up Carlton's."

"How in the world do you come to know that?"

"Young fellow from away? Looking for work? Any work? Not real handy? Who else would you be?"

"Who else would I be?"

"That thing at Carlton's was a hell of a thing," he went on. "How did you manage that?"

I explained to him how the fueling hose had come to be torn out, told him about the spark, said how badly I felt about the trouble I'd made for Carlton, who seemed to be a nice guy.

"He can afford to be a nith guy," my passenger said. "Don't worry about Carlton. Carlton's fine. You could blow a tank up on him every week, he'd never feel it. That thtation he's got? Goddamned gold mine. Here we are."

We had arrived at the stateline store in Bernardston where the old fellow bought his lottery tickets. I cut the engine, left the car, and went around to open the other door. My hitchhiker reached up for my hand. I took his and helped pull him out of the car and onto his feet. I handed him his stick. Then we went into the store and up to the counter.

"Hello, Shep," said the woman at the register.

"Hello, Eloise," said my passenger. "Got a couple of winners for me and my friend?"

"Sure do, Shep," said the clerk. "I've been saving them for you." She smiled at us. She took two tickets from the dispenser on her counter and accepted my rider's two dollars: a one-dollar bill and four quarters. He handed one of the tickets to me.

"That's okay," I said. "I'll buy my own."

"Hell, no, you won't. Leatht I can do, you driving me all over hither and yon."

"Twenty-five million seems like a lot for half an hour's driving."

"We ain't back yet. And, you underthtand, it's pothible we won't win the fifty million. That's pothible. Ain't it, Eloise?"

"It's possible," said Eloise.

· · · · · · ·

"Where were you, when you were overseas," I asked. We were on the road again, on our way back toward Brattleboro.

"I told you. Franth."

"Yes, but where in France?"

"God, I don't know. They didn't tell us nothing. All we thaw was a lot of flat brown country and villages all beat to shit by the shells. Looked like big brick piles. We didn't know how anybody could ever live there again, but I guess they do."

"Did you fight?" I asked him. "Well, of course you did. You were wounded."

"I didn't fight much," he said. "Didn't have time. After I was hit, I was in the rear. Learned to one-hand it, sat on my ath, helped to take care of the horses, played thtud poker with the medics. Did—I don't know—not much. After the armistith, we just waited to be thent home. Waited a long goddamned time, too."

"The armistice," I said.

"The armistith. I remember that, all right. Never forget it. I don't thuppose anybody who was over there will. We were in camp in a railroad yard, and all of a thudden here came a train just barreling. Highballing. Wide open, going east. And we could see it was full of guys in high thilk hats, and every kind of generals and other officers: brass and ribbons by the furlong in there. And all of them heading east, heading for the front. And our thergeant thaid, 'Boys, the war's over.' And we athked him how he knew, and he said, 'Boys, when you thee the generals and the politicians and them going *toward* the fight, you know the shooting hath thtopped.' He was right, too. November Eleven, nineteen-eighteen."

We had crossed the state line and were passing through downtown Brattleboro. I looked to my right and saw my passenger had gone to sleep on me. What had the woman in the store called him? Sid? Sam? Shep. It was Shep. Shep began gently to snore.

The poor old guy. At his age, destitute, hitchhiking like a kid. If he was draftable in 1917, he was born in the eighteen-nineties, maybe the eighties. That made him eighty-plus. Not an easy eighty, either: that arm, those teeth, that stoop, that stick. He's been pretty knocked around by life, hasn't he? What about me? Have I been knocked around by life? Not much. Will I be? I don't know. Am I being? I don't know.

What is his life? Every week, or whatever the interval is, he goes down to Bernardston to get his ticket. What else? Does he have a family? Is he alone? Am I? Will I always be?

I rolled down my window. The smell of whatever filthy stuff old Shep had been drinking was coming off him like a vapor. The rush of fresh air into the car woke him. He sat up and looked at me, looked ahead.

"Right there," he said. "Right in there. Thlow down."

I turned us into the Sno-White Cabins, an old-style motor court, long gone today, on Route 5 as you left Brattleboro going north. The Sno-White was not posh. It needed paint, it needed shingles. What it really needed was a good three-alarm fire. I stopped in the weed-grown concrete courtyard.

Shep opened his door. "Thankth again," he said.

"Don't you want me to run you up to Putney?" I asked him. "I can take you back to where you started."

"This ith where I thtarted."

"A motel?"

"I live here."

"In a motel? Isn't that expensive?"

"Not thith one."

"You must rent a cabin," I said. "That's expensive."

"I don't rent it."

"Who does, then?"

"You do, thon," said Shep. "State pays the rent. This here's a Deadbeat Hotel."

"I guess I didn't know about deadbeat hotels."

"You got your life ahead of you," said Shep. "You'll learn." He climbed out of the car and got his stick from the rear. He bent to look in at me. He patted his shirt pocket. "Don't lose your ticket," he said.

"I won't."

"Thee you don't. You show up at the lottery office to claim your fifty million and you don't have your ticket, they ain't going to pay off. They just flat won't do it."

"I'll hang onto it tight," I said. "Good luck."

"Luck," said Shep.

· · · · · · ·

Somebody knocking on the front of Minerva. Six a.m. I rolled out of my bunk in my shorts and stumbled to the door. On the cabin's front porch, a tall fellow with a bandana tied around his head, pirate-fashion, and wearing painter's coveralls festive with red, white, and blue spatters, as though somebody had run the American flag through a meat grinder, shaken the pieces up in a basket, and then shot them at him out of a cannon.

"You ready?" this specimen asked me.

"For what?"

"*'For what?'* Go to work. I thought you'd be ready."

"Who are you?"

"I'm Melbourne."

The name meant nothing to me. "Who?" I asked.

"*Who?* Are you looking for work, or ain't you?"

"I am."

"You afraid of heights?" He nodded toward his truck, idling in front of the cabin, two ten-foot extension ladders rattling gently on a rack above the bed.

"Not that I know of," I said.

"*Not that you know of.* If you are, we'll find out pretty quick. Jump in." He turned to leave the porch.

"Give me a minute," I said. "I'm not dressed."

"It don't matter to me if you are or if you ain't dressed," said Melbourne. "You ain't my type."

"Let me make myself a cup of coffee, at least," I said.

"Coffee's all made," said Melbourne. "Let's go."

So began what I guess you could call the adventure of my life. Not much of an adventure if you were on the Western Front, but mine nevertheless. Not everyone gets to live in history. I went to work for Melbourne. We found I didn't mind heights—rather enjoyed them, in fact. I waited daily for the calamity and failure that seemed to follow me to appear and do their work. They didn't.

Instead, I got to know Melbourne and his family. (For a little while, that winter, I lived with them.) I got to know his daughter. By and by, I got to know his daughter's friends. One friend in particular, home for Christmas.

"I don't get it about you," she said. "You're not related to anybody. You don't know anybody. Nobody knows you. Why are you even here?"

"I dropped from the sky."

"I believe it."

"Aren't you glad I did?" I asked her.

"Well, I'm not sorry," she said. "Or, not yet."

She's still not sorry. That is, I don't guess she is. It's been some time since I asked.

· · · · · · ·

"How did you happen to look me up, in the first place?" I asked Melbourne one time.

"*Happen?*" said Melbourne. "I didn't *happen* to. I heard you were looking for work. I'd had Danny, there, but then he went to Florida. Right around the same time, I got that big inn job in Newfane. I had to have somebody right now. I heard about you."

"From whom?"

"*From whom?* An old fellow I know. Knew you, he said. You picked him up."

"You mean Shep? The veteran?"

"That's right, Shep. The rest? I don't know. Shep, a vet?"

"He was in World War One. In France. He told me all about it."

"*He told you?*" said Melbourne. "I bet he did. France? Hah. A vet? Hah. Shep's no vet. What war would have him? With that arm?"

"But he lost it in the war."

"He lost it, all right," said Melbourne. "Years ago. What it was, Shep showed up for work at Simpson's mill one day, drunk as a skunk. Fell into the shingle-chopper. A disabled vet? Shep? That's a good one."

"How did he know where you'd find me, though?" I asked Melbourne. "I never told him where I lived."

"One thing about Shep," said Melbourne, "he may not be the brightest, but he don't miss much. I give him that."

· · · · · · ·

A golden afternoon in October: surely one of the last perfect days. I got back to Camp Artemis after working with Melbourne to find my Aunt Grace and Uncle Ted, returned from their travels, sitting on the front porch of Athena surrounded by their baggage. I left my car and went to greet them. Uncle Ted waved to me but stayed where he was. Aunt Grace, however, got to her feet and came to the edge of the porch, her normally beatific smile made at least twenty-five percent more beatific by six months in Nepal, her cloud of fine, perfectly white hair radiant in the warm sunlight. She put her palms together and bowed, smiling, to me.

"Namaste," she said.

Canyon Mouth

MELISSA BRODER

Have we figured out what's wrong with the world yet

and tossed it away laughing into a cauldron

of sugar, blood, and heat, and left the cauldron

bubbling on the suffering inferno

saying *fuck it* to the smoke, *just let it cook,*

it might just need to cook a little bit more

and taken one dog each out to the mountains

for a little elemental air and courage?

I don't know why I never do that anymore.

Each time I went out to the mountains, they stood

as evidence I should go on, the higher

I climbed, the more I forgot about that worldly broth,

This is how we stay alive, I said to myself,

although later I forgot, and to my dog

who didn't understand the language

but knew it somehow already by heart.

The Second Singularity

ALAN LIGHTMAN

NEURALNET #oooooooooooo On: *If we-thou may: The First Singularity, in which computers would become as intelligent as human beings, was conjectured in 1993 by Vernor Vinge and actualized in 2078. Except for the Damasio Effect, still unexplained, in which certain random processes in human neural networks and the resulting creativity injunctions could not be duplicated by machines. The Second Singularity was conjectured in 2122 by Sylvie Yu, shortly after the widespread implementation of neuralnet implants. According to Professor Yu's hypothesis, a large number of human brains connected to each other via the grid might reach a critical point, the so-called Second Singularity, from which would emerge some kind of "global consciousness." How many human brains, each acting like a single neuron in a vast mega brain, would be needed for S2? Would S2 occur gradually or all at once? Or perhaps not at all.* Neuralnet #oooooooooooo Off.

Eight o'clock. The neon lights burned weirdly in the thick greasy air. Astrid shoved her way through the street, pushing past hawkers and squatters and dazed gridheads sprawled against storefronts, until she neared the alley that led to her third-floor apartment. Shards of glass crunched under her boots. For a year, she'd been telling herself that she would move out of this neighborhood. But she liked being a big fish in a small filthy pond.

The smell of pork and onions reminded her that she was

hungry. At a fast food store on the corner, she paused and studied the flashing menu, then ordered a couple of coffees and veggie sandwiches. She was going to try to coax her boyfriend Chao into eating healthy tonight. For a moment, she thought that she might use her suppressor code to trick the computer and get the food free, as she sometimes did. It was too easy.

"I've got some sandwiches from Lala's," she said as she walked into the apartment. Chao was sitting on the couch and holding a cola, his head back, connected. He wasn't drinking the cola; he was just holding it, as if he'd forgotten it was in his hand. She walked over to the couch and gave him a quick kiss. "Want to eat?"

Chao didn't say anything.

Astrid checked on the dog, then went to her room and took off her boots. Despite the long day and the hunger, she was revved. She swallowed a couple of relax pills, ran through the channels on the digital screen, and changed into her lounging clothes. Still, she was jumpy. Somewhere outside, a siren wailed. She might invite Chao into her bed tonight. She hadn't decided. From the look of him on the couch, he wasn't going to disconnect any time soon, and she didn't want him in her bed while connected, naked or not. Once like that three months ago had been once too many.

In the small dining area, she put the food on the table. She sat down and began eating. "Join me?" she said.

"Later," murmured Chao. "I'm busy."

"I think you should eat something." She tasted the coffee, spit it out, and got a beer from the fridge. Then she felt the familiar tiny buzz in her head that meant someone was neuralnetting her.

Neuralnet #48074866712 On Restricted: *Hi.*

Neuralnet #85928572018 On Restricted: *Hi Lana. Could we talk in a half hour?*

Sure. But I do want to talk to you about something.

I really can't talk now. I'm eating dinner. I should have disconnected.

It's about Chao. Is he there at the moment? He's on the couch, isn't he?

Neuralnet #38593858206: On Restricted: *I'm on, too, ladies. Are we out on the town, or at home tonight? Astrid, we've been waiting to talk to you. For a couple of months. We're concerned.*

I'm going to disconnect. I just want a few quiet minutes to eat dinner.

Please don't disconnect. It's just the three of us. Astrid, we love you. You know that. We've wanted to talk to you. Please, just for a couple of minutes. [Pause] You can't stay with this guy. Sanjay was perfect for you. We won't go on about Sanjay, OK? But Chao. The way he is. We care about you. We hardly see you since you've been with him.

Thank you. I care about me, too. You don't know Chao. You met him just once. Maybe twice. He loves me. [Pause] He is the way he is.

Isn't that the point? You could have anybody. Look at him. Chao's a gridhead.

Don't call him that.

He doesn't do anything all day.

You don't know that.

You've told us yourself. When we saw him at Dave's, he looked like a freaking zombie. His face was cakey white. He could barely talk. Don't you remember? He embarrassed you. He embarrassed all of us. Astrid, we care about you. You could have anybody. Chao's a gridhead.

Some women just want a man who will lie down and keep his mouth shut.

I can't believe you said that, Lana. Astrid, Lana didn't mean that.

Thank you for caring about me. Goodnight, Lana. Goodnight Mara.   Neuralnet #85928572018 Off.

· · · · · · ·

After finishing dinner, Astrid put Chao's sandwich on the table in front of the couch. She glanced at him. His eyes were partly rolled back, and a little stream of spittle dribbled from the corner of his mouth. "Goodnight," she said and went into her room and closed the door. She took off her clothes and pulled the covers over her head. With her neuralnet off, she allowed herself to think. She closed her eyes, but she was still thinking. After taking another relax pill, she fell asleep.

· · · · · · ·

When Astrid went into the kitchen the next morning, Chao was still on the couch. She made some coffee. "How are you feeling?" she said. "You never get a good sleep when you stay connected all night."

"I'm OK," said Chao. "I'm used to it. I like it."

"I was wondering," said Astrid. "You're not connected right now, are you?"

"Not this minute."

"I was wondering. Look at yourself in the mirror."

"What for?"

"Please. Just do it."

Chao got up from the couch and walked barefoot to the mirror near the front door. "And?"

"Look at your eyes. And your face. Do you see how you look? You look out of it."

Chao got closer to the mirror and stared at himself.

"Don't take this the wrong way," said Astrid, "but I think you could disconnect more. It's not good to stay on the grid as much as you do."

"You never mentioned that before," he said.

"Well. Maybe it's time to mention it. I'm mentioning it now. You're not doing yourself any good being connected all day and all night."

Chao stood back from the mirror, stared at himself, got close again. He did some jumping jacks. Then he looked at himself again. "Maybe you're right," he said.

"I think I'm right," she said.

"Yep. I do look kind of pale."

"You could try disconnecting a little each day. Start with an hour. See how that feels. Then maybe you could do more."

Chao was still looking at himself in the mirror. "I think you're right. But I do want to be connected when S2 comes. You should be, too."

"There's a good center across the river I heard about," said Astrid. "They give people strategies. There's another one down by the transport station."

"That's an idea. It won't be easy."

They began discussing various plans Astrid had heard about. There was a plan where you disconnected for an hour in the evening, during dinner. There was another plan where you disconnected for an hour in the morning, before breakfast, and a half hour after lunch. There was one where you alternated twenty-minute intervals.

"I don't think I'd like the morning plan," said Chao. "There's too much news and other stuff in the morning."

"Of course," said Astrid. "Find something that suits you. You're in the driver's seat."

"Yep. I'm in the driver's seat." He sat down on the couch.

Astrid leaned over and touched him on the shoulder. She swept up the crumbs from his sandwich and went to the toilet. "Have a nice day," she said as she left.

Walking down the stairs, even before she got to the street, she heard the chanting outside. It had been like that every day for the last year. "S2. God is near. Nothing to fear. S2." Throngs of people wearing crimson robes flowed by her alley. The bottoms of the robes were soiled with the grime of the street. Some of the women carried babies newly implanted. The crowds had gotten larger in the last few months.

Neuralnet #59382049811 On: *Join in the glory, fellow travelers of the U-NI-VERSE. Prepare for the cosmic awakening. Prepare for the Oneness. Prepare to meet God.*

Frowning, Astrid turned off her neuralnet. To get to the opposite side of the street, she had to zigzag through the crowd. Nobody slowed a single step for her. Everyone was looking straight ahead at some invisible point on the horizon. Then Astrid headed for the transport station. On the levitrain, a heavyset man smiled at her. Astrid could tell he was trying to neuralnet her and annoyed she wasn't on the grid. He leaned over and said, "A pain, aren't they? The marchers."

"It's a free country," said Astrid.

"I think the whole thing's a hoax," said the man. He leaned his head back.

When Astrid got out of the train, another group of people

wearing white robes stood in front of the building. They had their own priest. "Soon, soon, soon," they chanted. "Prepare for immortality. Prepare for infinity. It will be soon."

Astrid went to Level Seven of the building, where a dozen other Suppressors were milling about on the glassy floor waiting for their codes for the day. For security, all neuralnets on Level Seven had to be off. Astrid mentally checked hers again. In fact, she was off grid most of the time, like all the Suppressors. They had to guard their thoughts. Astrid looked up at the global digital screen suspended from the ceiling. Every second, new points lit up, more brains connecting to the grid.

A man and a woman she didn't recognize stood next to her eating donuts and also looking up at the screen. "A lot of newbies in Nepal today," the woman said.

The man grunted. "Dumb Hindu breeders. I'll bet one of us gets Nepal today."

"I don't know anybody in Nepal," said the woman. "I got part of Mexico last week. Made me feel a little . . . I know people in Mexico City."

"So?" said the man. "Did any of them croak after you suppressed them?"

"A few hundred."

"That's a tiny percentage."

"Yes. But still."

"The way I look at it," said the man, "people spend too much time on the grid anyway." The man stood back from the woman, and his face suddenly changed. "Selma, you're not having qualms, are you?"

"No," the woman said quickly. She looked around. "No, no." Then she saw Astrid. "I didn't mean anything," she said to Astrid.

"No worries from me," said Astrid.

"I really didn't," said the woman. "I suppress whoever they give me."

"You don't have to explain anything to me," said Astrid. "I don't give a shit. They pay us. That's it for me."

"They do," said the man.

"I'm not political," said Astrid. "If the Viceroy and his friends want to stall S2 for whatever reasons, that's their business. They can run the show as long as they want. They pay me, I suppress. Period."

"Right," said the man. "My brother's been out of work for six months. We're lucky."

"You bet we are," said Astrid. She looked again at the digital screen. "One funny thing."

"What?" said the man.

Astrid wasn't saying anything that wasn't obvious. "Haven't you noticed that no matter how many people we get off the grid, more and more are getting on? The screen just gets brighter and brighter. It's tons brighter than it was a year ago."

The man studied Astrid.

"But so what?" said Astrid. "We get paid. Let the muckety-mucks worry about what they want to worry about. I think the whole thing's a hoax anyway. Nothing's going to happen. Fine by me. I can live like this a long long while."

The man nodded. "Here we go," he said. "I'm on for Hong Kong."

· · · · · · ·

At home that night, Astrid asked Chao whether he'd gotten to the center.

"Tomorrow," said Chao.

Two days later, she asked him again. "I'm working up to it," he said. "This isn't easy you know."

A week later, he was waiting for her at the door when she got home. "I did it," he said. He showed her his connection log. He'd disconnected for forty minutes that afternoon.

"That's something," said Astrid. "But you can do better."

A few days later, Chao said, "I've got a routine going now. Forty minutes at 4'clock. Four to four-forty. In two weeks, I'll get up to an hour. Then I'll go from there."

"You're on your way," said Astrid. "You look better. Also, you're getting out of the house."

Chao looked at himself in the mirror. "Yep. I do look better." He sat down at the dining room table and began eating the food Astrid had brought. "Everybody at the center is talking about S2," he said between bites. "There're people who think it's coming soon, and they don't want to be disconnected when it does."

"That sounds to me like an excuse to get off the program," said Astrid. "Nobody knows anything. My money is on it's not happening at all."

"Maybe, and maybe not," said Chao. "People at the center say they can feel something in their heads. Something different. I feel it."

"What are you talking about?" said Astrid, putting some food out for the dog.

"I can't describe it. Like wind going past my head. Like I'm flying. People at the center say that's the start of it. And then we're all going to dissolve into one person, and we're going to be really really smart, and we're going to be able to see all the stars and the other planets, and God. We're going to see God."

Astrid got a beer from the fridge and sat down next to Chao. "Just keep up on your program," she said. She turned toward him. There was a little color in his face, and he didn't look bad in his sports T-shirt. "Would you mind disconnecting for fifteen minutes?" she said. "I know you've done your forty minutes for the day. Just fifteen minutes more?"

"OK," said Chao. "Fifteen minutes."

Astrid took him into her room.

· · · · · · ·

It was the next week that Astrid first noticed soldiers at the street corners. She couldn't tune in to anything they were thinking. The soldiers just stood there in pairs watching people.

There were soldiers on Level Seven, too. "What's this about?" Astrid asked one of them, a tall man who limped as he slowly circled the room. He didn't answer.

"What does the Viceroy think we're going to do?" said Philip, one of Astrid's colleagues.

"We're not the rest of them." Astrid looked up at the digital screen.

· · · · · · ·

Astrid went on a trip. Once or twice a month, she'd been assigned to relocate for a couple of days. It had something to do with the networks where she inserted the suppressor viruses. She didn't ask questions. But the trips were getting more frequent. This one was seven time zones away. At night, she went out for a few drinks. She sat at the bar. Most of the customers were lying in reclining chairs, connected, their heads back, their drinks sitting untouched on the tables.

"Let's have some music," said Astrid. "Liven things up."

The bartender gave a bitter laugh. "They don't want any music," he said. "No sir. My place is turning into a hotel for gridheads." He poured himself a drink. "They don't talk. They don't move around much. They buy one round of drinks and that's it. And I'll tell you something. They don't take baths either." Two soldiers with stun guns walked in and sat at a table. "Last night, the gridheads were here until two in the morning," said the bartender. "After that, they slept on the sidewalk in front. Dozens of them. The whole city's turning into gridheads."

Astrid nodded. "It's hurting business," she said.

"Damn right," said the bartender. "I could murder the whole bunch of them."

Neuralnet #97950546327 On Restricted: *Hi.*

"Excuse me for a moment," Astrid said to the bartender.

Neuralnet #85928572018 On Restricted: *Hi.*

When are you coming home?

In a couple of days.

Can you hear the hum?

What hum?

There's a hum. It's coming over the net. People are talking about it. It's on the news.

I haven't heard any hum.

That's 'cause you're not connected enough. It's happening. S2 is happening.

How's your program going?

Good.

I've got to go. See you in a couple of days.

Neuralnet #85928572018 Off.

When Astrid left the bar later that night, there were more soldiers on the streets.

Crowds of people gathered in a grassy area holding candles. She turned on her neuralnet briefly and heard a humming sound. Maybe it was just a thousand people thinking thoughts all at once. That's probably what the hum was. Across the street, two soldiers were putting a woman in a truck.

· · · · · · ·

On Thursday, Astrid arrived at her apartment at four-fifteen in the afternoon.

Chao was sitting on the couch, his head back. "What are you doing?" she shouted. She shook him by the shoulders. Chao sat up suddenly, pain on his face from abrupt disconnection. "You're supposed to be disconnected between four and four-forty," she shouted.

Chao rubbed his head, then went to the sink and splashed water on his face. "It won't happen again," he said.

"You're a fucking gridhead," said Astrid. "You're pathetic."

"Don't talk to me like that," said Chao. "I'm a human being."

"You're a fucking gridhead."

Chao went into his room. A few minutes later, he came out with his duffel bag. "I'll tell you something, Ms. Superior," he said. "You're going to miss out. You go ahead and keep doing your dirty business. But you're going to miss out. You're not going to be part of it. It's coming very very soon, and you won't be part of it. I won't feel sorry for you either. And I'll tell you something else. I'm not on the plan anymore. I'm staying connected as much as I damn well please."

Chao sat down on the couch.

Later that night, Astrid was awakened by the sound of sirens. She went out.

Hundreds of soldiers carrying guns stood by their vehicles. Trucks rumbled down the street. The marchers were out, too, shouting and chanting. There were others sitting quietly, connected, not the usual gridheads but ordinary people in nice clothes, sitting outside in the middle of the night. Children lay down next to their parents fully awake. Some people had gone out on the river in open boats and stared up at the black sky.

Astrid turned on her neuralnet.

Neuralnet #48739573629 On: *S2 is coming tonight. Are we ready?*

Neuralnet #49305738925 On: *Yes, yes, we're ready. I'm ready. I'm lifting. Beautiful. I see a planet from outer space. I'm out of my body.*

A man ran past Astrid, bleeding.

Neuralnet #60385603728 On: *The sins of humanity are over. Soon we are one. Gaia God.*

More sirens and shouting. The marchers were running now. Astrid sat down on the sidewalk next to a gridhead. The woman was trembling, and her skin glowed ochre in the pale neon light. Astrid felt a humming, which turned louder and louder. Then, silence.

La Frontera Forever

GABINO IGLESIAS

WHAT HAPPENS WHEN YOU CROSS la frontera is that you leave a place to enter a void. You vacate a known reality and change it for something that you have to force yourself to believe, to accept, to understand.

What happens when you cross la frontera is that you shed un pedazo grande of your identity and become a different thing, something that's part apparition, part useless flesh, and part broken memories. You abandon familia, amigos, lenguaje, and the streets you know for a place where you have no rights and are not even considered a citizen, a country in which you will live like a stowaway rat, always afraid of being discovered. So you change. You morph. Te vuelves otra cosa. You start speaking English fast in hopes that your brown skin will be ignored if you at least communicate well. You dress yourself with the comics you read and the books you hated in school and the movies you've watched since you were a kid and that thing becomes el nuevo tu. You cover your tatuajes and learn that people on the streets will remember you only if you speak Spanish in their presence. You do everything in your power to become a gringo, to fit in, to become as unnoticeable as the cracks on the sidewalks. Then you start walking with less confidence because everything is mysterious and new and scary and you never feel bienvenido.

What happens when you cross la frontera is that la frontera keeps a piece of you, cuts you inside, hasta el hueso, where you can't heal yourself. It slashes you in places no blade or bullet can reach and cripples you in ways you don't understand. Cruzar la frontera fucks you over en formas que no sabías que podías ser jodido. What happens when you cross la frontera is that your body becomes a magnet for the bad stuff that has piled up all along that awful dividing line.

Muerte.

Destrucción.

Desesperación.

Olvido.

La nada infinita.

La noche eterna full of screams.

Crossing la frontera is like crossing a swamp because you end up covered in unpleasant shit no matter what you do. La frontera is a place of crying espíritus. It's a place of almas perdidas y en pena, all of them looking for a way back, for a way to undo what happened, for a path back to their loved ones and their known places and a time before what turned out to be an awful decision was made.

La frontera is a place where miedo seeps into your bones and the silence you're forced to keep allows the cries of dead children to enter your soul and break you in half like a dry twig. La frontera is a place where los huesos de los muertos are never buried deep enough and the pain of broken familias and la sangre de los inocentes has mixed with the plants and the air and the soil. All this darkness is what gives el río its peculiar smell and green color. Some things have a bottom but they are bottomless, and el río is one of them because a dark universe hides in its greenish depths. The infinite darkness that hides in that flowing jade vein is what makes white men with guns pull the trigger even when the figure moving under the crosshairs is a woman or a child.

What happens when you cross la frontera is that you shatter, you stop being you and turn into a new person that belongs nowhere, that has no home, no roots. Going back is impossible and moving forward is like jumping into a cave and hoping that it's not too deep, that the rocks don't mangle you too much, and that el monstruo that waits for you en la oscuridad is not too hungry.

What happens when you cross la frontera is that you have to do whatever it takes to survive, and that's what pushes you into a life of crime. You need money to survive and washing dishes or mowing lawns are easy gigs to get but they don't pay enough. In this country, fairness is a concept and nothing more. Los pinches gringos will send dinero to Africa and will pay thousands of dollars to chop their cat's huevos off and remove their nails, but they won't pay you a fair amount for painting their fucking mansiones and, if you complain, te llaman a la migra. Pinches hijueputas. Why the fuck should you do stuff in this country that you would never have done back home? Why should you smell like the shit you have to clean when you used to roll around with chingos de lana in your pocket? Thinking about that either makes you look for something different or breaks you again.

What happens when you cross la frontera is that you want to clean up, find a good job somewhere, meet a beautiful, sweet girl. You want the American Dream. But fuck all that. The American Dream is as false as the meat in your one-dollar burger and the canned laughter you hear on television. And it's even worse for you. You have no skills and no diploma and no friends and no nada. You're a problem. Un ilegal más. A beaner. A television joke. A wetback. You're nothing but an issue brainless white politicians discuss from the safety of their offices. That's when any offer becomes salvation, any desperate move a solution, every bad idea something that gives you a bit of hope. That's when you realize that you will always live in a silent war and that anyone who's not from your patria can be your enemy at any moment. That's why you easily fall into selling rich white kids drugs while you pretend to work security at a bar.

Desperation leads to the gig at the door and the gig at the door leads to some money and the bills in your pocket lead to an apartment and a sense of accomplishment. You talk to Guillermo and he talks to a white college student who drives a shiny new BMW and asks you for $400 cash and leases a one-bedroom apartment under his name and hands you the key. "You pull any stunts, I'll have my friends find you. You don't want that to happen, amigo," he says. You smile, nod. Pinche gringo pendejo playing tough guy. You want to tell him, No mames, güey, while you grab him by the throat and slam his head against the pavement until his brain comes out his nose. You want to fill his stupid mouth with dirt so he can feel what many others feel as they try to cross la frontera and end up with their faces in the dirt as the sun devours the flesh of their backs. But you don't. You stay put and put all your strength on ignoring your desires. Instead of teaching the huevón a lesson, you take the keys he's holding out to you and enter your new casa for the first time ever. Then you put a mattress on the floor and a small television next to it. You put some food in the fridge and build your altar and start trying to convince yourself that it isn't so bad. Then you settle in somewhat and stay away from the leasing office, never check your mail, and get the fuck out of there for the entire day whenever they leave a note on the door saying someone will be entering the apartment to kill some cucarachas or check the batteries en los detectores de humo. You don't know it yet, but this vida de mentira, this hiding around, it starts turning you into a ghost, a transparency on two legs, a shadow that's not attached to anything solid. Then, when you notice, you also realize that being almost invisible is helpful and that your indistinctness is the only reason no one really notices you working the door at the bar and selling all sorts of overpriced pharmaceuticals to kids who think they're really cool.

You're in the corazón of a large city, completely exposed for hours to thousands of faces that come to 6th Street to drink and dance and try to fuck someone, but no one pays attention to you. You're a darker spot moving within a charco de sombra, just another brown face in a town where brown faces look out at you from every drive thru window and brown hands clean every car and a woman from a country south of the border cleans every mansion and every landscaping crew is full of guys who look just like you and every precious toddler at the park knows a bit of Spanish because his nanny only speaks Spanish when mommy and daddy aren't around.

What happens when you cross la frontera is that you don't know what's going to happen to you and you hustle harder than you ever hustled before and you pray to la Santa Muerte and ask for protección and do bad things that you convince yourself are not that bad because la frontera crossed your abuelos first and no one is really pinche ilegal because people can't be illegal and we're all atrapados en este puto mundo. Then you try to forget about everything that came before, you try to pretend like the familia and the women and the amigos and the laughter and the fear and the bodies and the money and the years are just not there and you focus on making money, staying alive, and being invisible. And the easiest way to be invisible is to be in front of a lot of eyes that don't give a shit about you being there.

Working at the club is the best way to make money and hide in plain sight. Most Mexicans come to this country and end up doing backbreaking work for fucking centavos because they're afraid of la migra and think being out in the open and having a visible job will lead to deportation. Al carajo eso. You do what you have to do and even learn to enjoy it a little because you can pay your bills and have plenty of pills at home and own a car and a gun and an iPod full of buena música and even have more than enough lana at home to replace the iPod some pinches mareros stole from you.

What sometimes happens when you cross la frontera is that you go to work the night after some assholes kidnapped you and chopped someone's head off right in front of you. Being there is weird and your butt clenches every time you think about walking to your car alone after all the rich white drunks have gone back to their homes and dorms, but it also makes you feel like life is already doing its thing and moving on. Because the thing about life is that time gets between facts and memories and as memories turn into what they are, facts start sliding back, moving into a space full of images from películas and skeletons from bad dreams and imagined monstruos and stuff that someone told you. That makes the fear lessen. Then you start thinking about the Russian cruising around in a car like a hungry predator looking for prey. You think about his gun spitting out justice and someone's head hitting the pavement with a loud thud and then blood running down into the gutter. Between that thought and the knowledge that la Santísima Muerte is watching your back, you give folks their drugs, stuff the money they hand over into your pocket before transferring it to the little box behind the bar, pop a few oxies, and walk to your car without looking back every two seconds while you wish for the call that will let you know que la muerte ha hecho su trabajo.

"La Frontera Forever" first appeared in different form in Gabino Iglesias' novel *Zero Saints* (Broken River Books, 2015)

Concord Free Press Interview

LEWIS HYDE

Lewis Hyde's singular curiosity leads him down unexpected paths, earning him a reputation as one of the finest non-fiction writers of our time. Defying easy categorization, his works *The Gift: Imagination and the Erotic Life of Property*, *Trickster Makes This World: Mischief, Myth, and Art*, and *Common as Air: Revolution, Art, and Ownership* are at once scholarly and wandering, personal and universal, and always fascinating. We interviewed him in his home in Cambridge, Massachusetts, on the same day his page proofs arrived for his latest book, *A Primer for Forgetting: Getting Past the Past*, from Farrar, Straus and Giroux.

Growing up, were you more inquisitive than other kids?

I doubt that. But my father was an optical physicist, and I came from a family of scientists—or a family where science mattered. So, if I had an interest in rocks or minerals or butterflies, it was supported by my family. I don't know if I was more inquisitive than others. But if I was inquisitive, it was honored.

Did your family move around a lot?

I was born in Cambridge, Massachusetts, and only lived in three other places that mattered. We lived for three years in England and six years in Connecticut and then four years in

Pittsburgh, Pennsylvania—then I went off to college at the University of Minnesota.

What do you consider the formative event of your early life?

When I was six or seven years old, I had a younger sister who died of viral encephalitis. She was eighteen months old, and we were living in England. People always say that children that young don't understand death. But, of course, it was a great rupture in my family, and it gave me a sense that people could disappear at any time. I think that sense is still with me.

Did your early interest in science keep going in college?

When I went to the University of Minnesota, I thought I would probably go into science of some kind. Happily, I got a D in Chemistry and then I moved to the Humanities. When my father taught Physics, he used to complain that nobody got a D in English and moved to the Physics department.

When did you become interested in writing?

At the University of Minnesota, I slowly gravitated toward the writers. I worked for the campus newspaper. And once every month there was a literary magazine that came out—sadly, called *The Ivory Tower*. But when I was there, the editor was Garrison Keillor. I was the editor after Garrison. So I got drawn into a bunch of other undergraduate writers—Jim Moore who was (and still is) a poet, Patricia Hampl who is still publishing, Garrison, and other young writers.

Who was teaching there, your mentors?

The writers at Minnesota then were Allen Tate and John Berryman. I never knew Tate, but I took classes from Berryman and he was sort of the on-campus poet. Sadly, at the time, he was still an active alcoholic. When I was in graduate school, he killed himself and this was upsetting to all of us. Many years later, I ended up writing an essay called "Alcohol & Poetry: John Berryman and the Booze Talking." I was working in the Cambridge City Hospital detox ward as a counselor. One night I was having trouble with one of the drunks, and the nurse said to me, "Don't get upset, Lewis, that's just the booze talking." As a writer, I was interested in this image, as if alcohol itself could speak. So my essay talks about Berryman's poetry, particularly *The Dream Songs*, as influenced by his having been an active alcoholic.

That must have been a tough essay to write.

I had been given these two experiences—the chance to know Berryman and the chance to work in the hospital. The essay just put the two experiences together.

From what we've read about your life, you have had a lot of odd jobs—besides working in the hospital.

My least favorite job was building grain bins in Minnesota. When a farmer buys a grain bin, it comes as a kit and you put it together. It's a circle of metal that you assemble like an Erector Set. That was a crummy job. Then I worked as an electrician in a mobile home factory, which I actually kind of enjoyed. You get to go to work and do something and by the end of the day something has been done. Also, I play the guitar, and there was a period when I made pocket money playing in bars. So yes, a series of odd jobs. When I was building grain bins, I thought if I put this much time into my writing, I could maybe get someplace.

Those sound like fairly solitary jobs. Did you find that solitude was really important when you were just beginning as a writer?

The other writer in Minnesota who was important to me was the poet Robert Bly. Bly wasn't at the University of Minnesota. He was in western Minnesota in Madison. But Robert always preached the gospel of solitude, which worked for him and worked for me as well. I don't think it works for everybody. But it was the case, for many years when I was beginning to write, that it was useful to me to find ways to be alone, even for a weekend or a week. So yes, solitude has been an important piece of my writing life.

And meeting Robert Bly was a turning point. This was the middle Sixties in Minnesota. I was involved in the anti-war movement, and we went to Washington, D.C., several times on buses. One of those times, I was on the bus playing my guitar, which was annoying everybody, and Robert was on the bus as well. Here was this somewhat older guy, and I guess none of us knew who he was. Then a couple months later, he came to the University of Minnesota to give a reading, and I figured out, "Oh, that's the guy I met on the bus." So those early days of being involved with a group of writers in Minnesota, in situations in which you were just thrown together, were very helpful to me.

In my new book, *A Primer for Forgetting*, there's a story about when I worked in the civil rights movement in 1964. I was in Mississippi as part of the Mississippi Summer Project or Freedom Summer, when three of the civil rights workers were murdered. So there's a lot to say about that summer. It was my first experience of living in a police state.

What did you take away from that experience?

I suppose how fragile democracy is. And how deep our problems with race are.

The way you've met important people in your life seems pretty coincidental. Has your life had a lot of serendipity in it?

Oh, I think all lives do, yes. I first came to the Boston area in the late 1970s, following a girlfriend who went off and found somebody else. But I had friends in Minnesota who were publishing a little poetry magazine called *The Lamp in the Spine*. There were exactly four people in Boston who subscribed to it, and I called them all up and said, "I'm new in town and I'm looking for somebody to have lunch with." One of them invited me to a lawn party in Arlington, where I met the woman who is now my wife. Another turned out to need a roommate, and I moved in with him. He was the guy who knew about Cambridge City Hospital and how to get a job there. Later, he knew a woman who had an apartment for rent, which many years later ended up being the house I bought in Cambridge.

This very house?

Yes, so my entire Cambridge life is based on serendipitous events.

Was one of the other two *Lamp of the Spine* **subscribers a complete psycho?**

No, just one from whom nothing happened.

Many descriptions of your work seem pretty reductive. Could you, in your own words, tell us what the commonalities are across all your books?

I have this phrase that I use a lot: *I'm interested in the public life of the imagination.* So *The Gift* is about the intersection between the creative life and the commercial world. *Trickster* is a similar intersection between the disruptive imagination and the cultures that wish they could remain stable. And *Common as Air* is about the cultural commons and the threats to it that we currently face with the desire to have all abstract intellectual property owned by somebody.

And I'm always interested in mythology. I come out of poetry, even if I'm not writing poems, and out of sort of mythic-poetic sensibility. So I'm interested in the myths and stories that motivate these different topics. *The Gift* begins with fairy tales that have gifts in them, as opposed to sociology about gifts or something more academic. And *Trickster* also begins with the mythology of the trickster. My new book, *A Primer for Forgetting*, begins with ancient stories about memory and forgetfulness, particularly stories about trying to imagine what happens to the memories of the dead. Is there a journey that the dead soul makes? Can the memories of the dead be preserved, or are they lost?

All of my books have mythological material in them. And I think of myths as true in the sense that they give you a pattern for thought and a vocabulary that is useful at any time and place. It helps you read the world as it's currently constituted, even if the myth is very old.

Mythology as a decoder for the modern world.

Yes.

Your work is deeply researched, but there's also a lot of personal narrative and meandering that goes on. A less gifted writer would have just laid out the facts and arguments. But you know how to tell fascinating stories. I think that's why so many writers are drawn to your work. You've said before that you write for all thinking humans. Did you set out to be a more approachable intellectual?

I guess, but I don't understand why one *wouldn't* do that.

Some scholars can't.

In literature departments, people tend to be drawn to literature because they love it, but then they write in a way that is not lovable. I want to write, always, in a way that invites the reader in and assumes a connection between me and the reader. As a writer, you have to have a sense of when you're boring people. And if you don't have that sense, well, you probably shouldn't be writing. So, yes, I believe that stories engage the imagination. There are ideas and data in my books, but I tend to think that they always have to arise from a story that the reader can enter so that the data have a body.

You wrote *The Gift* during the pre-Internet era, obviously, and now the issue of how content is created, shared, modified, and valued has become even more complicated and fascinating.

I think that's one of the reasons *The Gift* has survived—it turned out that gift economies can flourish on the Internet, often in ways that they couldn't do before. And so people found actual cases that seemed to illustrate the liveliness of this model.

You were an early inspiration for the Concord Free Press, and your support has meant a lot to us. We've always described ourselves as a gift economy applied to publishing. Where do you see the CFP fitting into the larger picture of giving?

It's a nice instance of an invented gift economy. You found a cunning way to mine one vein of possible engagement—that people who care about literature write and work together to give the books away. Then as a consequence, readers give money to charities. It's a wonderful invention based on a simple idea.

Thanks, Lewis! One of the more fascinating parts for us is seeing the diverse ways that people give—and where they give.

In *The Gift*, I talk about individualism in a gift economy. There's a passage about children in a Native American community who get to create their identity by deciding who to give their gifts to. That is, a gift economy isn't necessarily a submersion of your individual identity. You express your identity by choosing to whom the gift goes. So your model is the same. People get the book, and then they choose what charity to give it to. There's a kind of self-expression in that, even as it's a gift economy.

We've often wondered how you know when you find an idea that's going to sustain the amount of energy, thought, and time that goes into writing one of your books.

I work very slowly, so it matters to me to be working on something that is not going to get easily exhausted—and is, in fact, usually a little bit mysterious. The book that I just finished on forgetfulness is a book about time and memory, as well as forgetfulness. Human beings live with all of these ideas, but they're still mysteries. Who knows what time is?

It's a wave. It's a particle.

[Laughs]. Yes, exactly. As for how I choose a topic, there has to be some emotional connection, some sense that this matters. Beyond that, I mean, I don't know how you decide when something is fascinating, but in fact some things are fascinating and others are not. So I try to watch for what fascinates me.

Do you keep resonant objects around you when you're writing? Things from nature, from your past? Things that people give you? Do you keep those near where you write?

A little bit, yes. In my study right now, I have a little work of art that William Kentridge gave to me. When Kentridge was creating *Triumphs and Laments* on the Tiber River in Rome, his crew made small laser-cut images of some of the silhouettes and he gave me one. Mostly, I like to have things around me that have been given to me, and often they're beautiful.

Is Trump a trickster? Or maybe a dirty trickster?

When people ask me that, I always say *no*, for two reasons. First, in the ancient mythology of the trickster, this character's never in the middle of the world. He's never the leader. He's an edge figure, always at the border of the town or at the gates of the city or at the edge of the firelight. And second, tricksters are funny. The trickster stories are humorous, telling them often makes people laugh. They're scatological and rude, and Mr. Trump has no sense of humor. He's a completely humorless man, and so that also means that he doesn't belong to this mythology.

Who do you consider a modern-era trickster?

Tricksters tend to be the people who are able to take you to the places where the culture is suffering and find the kind of humor that lets you look at the suffering and live with it— and find ways to change it. I always thought of someone like Richard Pryor, a humorist who managed to get into the gears of where things are stuck and lubricate them. I haven't been thinking about this for a long time, so I can't come up with a more current example. But there will always be a vein of artistic practice and artists trying to reimagine the world—and change the categories that are not working well anymore.

Looking to the future, what do you see as the biggest threat to the creativity and openness that you've explored in your work?

The main threat is that the market triumphalism that we've now been living with for several decades has made it harder and harder for young artists to go through that period in which they learn what their talents are, how heavily they can press on them, how many drafts of the first novel they have to do. I always think that after college, a young artist needs maybe ten years of being able to live cheaply and be supported by friends while he or she gets the work made and out into the world. The big centers where people used to do this—in New York City or San Francisco—are prohibitively expensive. And also the attacks on public funding for the arts have worked so well it's hard for artists to find support during those periods.

The other challenge—and I'm conflicted about this topic—is that the interest in race and class and gender has become so heavily politicized that I think it's hard for artists who are working in some other way. My example would be someone like James Turrell. Turrell is an artist whose work is entirely about light. It has nothing to do with race, class, and gender. Again, this is not opposing work that takes on those topics. But simply saying that there are other realms that are less obvious and less supported now. I think it's hard for upcoming artists to feel the freedom to explore something that's never been explored.

What advice would you give a young creative soul right now?

Have courage. If I look back at my own life, it was helpful to live for certain periods where the rent was very cheap. So know that you don't need to go to the supposed centers of culture to do your work. And find role models you love. I sometimes think every young artist should find an older artist whose work matters to them and, in some way, do a favor for that person or that work. An example would be when Bob Dylan was young, he fell in love with Woody Guthrie's work. But he didn't just fall in love with it. He went to New York City, found Woody Guthrie in the hospital, sang songs to Woody Guthrie, memorized all of his songs, and wrote a song for him. It's a kind of apprenticeship—doing something for the person who matters to you.

When I was young, I translated two books of Pablo Neruda's because I like Neruda's poetry. So I put myself in service to the previous generation. At some point, you have to break away also, but I think it's a useful kind of apprenticeship when you're young—find something you love and do a favor for it.

Oh, Canada

RUSSELL BANKS

MALCOLM SAYS HE DOESN'T GET IT.

Vincent is changing cards again and letting the camera cool, and Diana and Sloan remain silent. For all Fife knows they have fallen asleep. Which is fine by him. Same with Renée. None of this would make sense to Renée or have the slightest importance or relevance anyhow.

Fife calls Emma's name. No answer. He calls it again. Where is she? He didn't notice her leaving, although he probably wouldn't have, he was so absorbed in what he was saying. But there must have been a flash of light cutting through the darkness when she left the room. If she left it.

Fife asks Malcolm did Emma go out while he was talking, and Malcolm, after a significant pause, says yes.

Fuck! Renée, please go to Madame Fife, he tells his nurse, speaking in French, and tell her that I can't continue unless she is present.

Renée points out that Madame Fife may not wish to be disturbed.

Fife doesn't care. Bring her back. If Emma is not able to listen to his story, then it will never get told. It's too late for him to try telling it over again—to her, to himself, to anyone who cares to listen. He's a dying man, doped against the pain of his dying and the disease that is poisoning and eating and digesting his body, turning it into excrement.

Renée says that she will go to Madame Fife's office and try to explain to her what he has said.

Fife turns to Malcolm, You don't get it? What don't you get? Does what I'm saying not make sense? He fears there is something terribly wrong with the way he is describing his beginnings, that somehow no one is hearing him the way he hears himself. Maybe it's the meds, the sickness, the fatigue and weakness. Maybe he's remembering one thing and saying a different thing, as if everything he remembers actually happened to someone else, that Total Stranger, and not to Leonard Fife.

Malcolm says sure, sure, some of it makes sense. Not all. But it doesn't matter, they'll edit it so that it ends up a coherent, lucid narrative. You know how it's done, he says. You know better than anyone.

Fife wants an example of something that doesn't make sense, something that Malcolm doesn't get. Because to Fife it all connects. It all leads gradually step by step to who he was when he came to Canada in '68 and became the man who, now that he is dying, they want to interview so they can make a documentary film to be shown on national television to all Canada. How can Malcolm *not* get it?

The clothes, for instance, Malcolm says. The stuff you lifted from the menswear store. They're all winter clothes. It's like you're running away to Canada in 1958, instead of Cuba. I mean, Pendleton shirts? Gloves?

That was later, when I was traveling from Virginia to Vermont, and my suitcase got lost in transit between Richmond and my connecting flight in Washington. Fife isn't sure if he confused the two journeys in the telling or Malcolm confused them in the hearing.

Malcolm tells him not to worry, it's a small thing. A minor detail. He'll probably cut it from the film anyhow. Not the part about Fife's dropping out of college in 1958 and running off to join Castro, though. That's interesting, because of how it prefigures Fife's filmmaking career. That's the kind of material they need more of, Fife's early politics and its gradual, growing connection to his art. Maybe Fife can follow that up by telling how his politics first showed up in his writing, now that they know that before he was a filmmaker he was a writer. Maybe Fife can talk a little more about his early writings, the novel he mentioned, for instance, and the poems. And the writers he liked back then. And how he became a draft-dodger in the States.

Out of the darkness Sloan suddenly speaks up. Speaking of writers, she likes the mention of Jack Kerouac and *On the Road*. An amazing book! Malcolm gave her a copy last month, and it blew her away, she says. What was it like, reading *On the Road* back when it was first published? It must've really blown Fife's mind to read it in America in the 1950s. That was like the McCarthy era, right? Korea? The Cold War and all that anti-communist stuff?

Diana interrupts her. Just let Malcolm ask the questions, dear.

Sorry. I'll keep it zipped.

Yes, dear. Keep it zipped.

Jesus! Maybe I should leave.

Please, you two, Malcolm says. Stay here, Sloan. I need you to do the sound. And Diana, lay off Sloan, will you? She's just trying to help. She's got a thing about Kerouac is all.

Yeah, right. You gave her the book, *On the Road*. Why? So she'd have a thing about the film director who turned her on to Kerouac? Please.

Don't start, Diana. It's just a fucking book.

Fife laughs. Yeah, Diana, it's just a fucking book. In answer to Sloan's question, he tells her that he doesn't remember what it felt like when he read *On the Road* back in 1958. He only remembers that he read it, because that summer his best friend, Nick Dafina, read it and told him that it reminded him of when he and Fife stole a car two years before and went on the road for six weeks before they got busted in Pasadena, California, when Nick, who was a good Catholic boy, went to confession and the priest he confessed to called the cops on them. And two years later, when first Nick and then Fife read the novel, they thought it was about them, instead of Sal Paradise and Dean Moriarty or Jack Kerouac and Neal Cassady, even though Leonard Fife and Nick Dafina were only sixteen when they went on the road and those other guys were in their mid-twenties and Kerouac when he wrote it was in his thirties.

The door to the hallway opens and for a second the blacked-out living room is illuminated, as Emma enters with Renée following her. Renée closes the door and drops the room back into darkness, except for the overhead spot on Fife's bald head.

In a barely audible voice, Emma says, This is hard on me, Leo. I know, I'm not the one who's sick, but Christ, this feels like some kind of post-mortem. And besides, you're exhausted. The meds are messing with your mind. You're confused, darling, and saying things that shouldn't be said on camera. Can't we stop this and maybe try again when you're feeling better?

I'm never going to feel better, you know that.

Malcolm says, A Catholic priest turned you and your friend in? That's true? I thought they weren't supposed to do that. He laughs and says that he doesn't know how much of all this to believe. This is getting more and more like a Werner Herzog film, like *Little Leo Wants to Fly* or something. Maybe Fife is making it all up, or inventing enough of it that in the end the whole thing is an invention, like a novel. Even Fife's name. Is his name really Leo Fife?

Vincent says, Okay, we're ready to rock 'n' roll. Papa's got a brand new card.

Fife says, Yes, Leonard Fife is really his given name.

Who gave it to you?

Fife ignores the question. It's more important to respond to Emma right now. I need you for this, he tells her. I'll never ask anything of you again. It's the only way I can finish my life with a clean conscience. My life since I was a boy has been a nightmare, a nightmare of my own making, that I'm finally trying to wake from. While I still can.

But why can't you unburden yourself, if that's what you're doing, alone with me? Privately. Why do you have to do it like this, in front of a camera?

Because I've spent most of my adult life behind the camera, asking questions off-camera, then editing my questions out, until all that remains are the answers I wanted heard and the images I wanted seen. Just as Malcolm is doing now. Fife says the only way he knows how to tell the truth is to sit himself in darkness in front of a camera, clip on a mic and start talking. Without the camera and the mic, without the darkness surrounding him, he would lie. He would try to make Emma love him more than she does. He would watch her face, especially her eyes. He would check out her body's reactions to his words, and he'd change his story. If he could see her, he'd lie. If he could see any of them, he'd lie. Even in darkness, talking only to Malcolm, Vincent, Diana and Sloan. Because he is so familiar with the medium, if they weren't sitting in same the room with him, he would still lie. He would try to make himself more attractive and interesting and lovable than he is. Emma is the only person who loves him for what he is, regardless of what he is. She's the only person Fife doesn't feel the need, the compulsion, to seduce. It's like a prayer, he says quietly. You don't lie when you pray.

Malcolm cuts in to say that he can dig Fife's point about the camera and mic and being in darkness, how it invites one to tell the truth in a way one wouldn't if one could see the camera and the person asking the questions. It's a technique, a process practically invented by Fife himself. For decades Fife has been able to get people to admit on camera things that they would never say otherwise. It's how he got Major Gordon to tell about the napalm tests in Gagetown. It's how he got the cannibals from Ontario to confess what really happened on the disastrous Arctic expedition to Banks Island. It's how he got Bishop

McCann to admit that he covered up for all those pedophile priests in Nova Scotia and Cape Breton.

Fife interrupts and asks Emma if he can start again.

She sighs and says, yes, go ahead. She'll stay with him until he's finished.

Malcolm suggests that Fife go back to that bit about him and his high school buddy, Nick Whatzizname, stealing a car and hitting the road like Jack Kerouac and Neal Cassady. He wants to know if the novel *On the Road* was an influence. Kerouac was French-Canadian, he says. Although in the book the Kerouac character, Sal Paradise, was not, he adds. Sal Paradise was American, a writer.

Malcolm claps his hands in front of the camera lens and says, Okay, here we go! April 1, 2017. Leonard Fife Interview. Montreal.

"Oh Canada" is an excerpt from a novel in progress.

Study for a Still Life

ELIZABETH SPIRES

In my room, a photo of you, ancient & praying.
And my young daughter, face upturned to mine,
   in a year I would call back.
And gingko leaves, gold fading to brown,
   in a bamboo bowl.
And small smooth stones washed up by waves,
   shining on a bone-white plate.
And a gray-green hummingbird's nest,
   both weighty & weightless in my hand.
And a black & white scroll where a traveler
   ascends into a realm of stone & air.
The ten thousand things of a life! Here, in this room.

Breakage & juncture. So much breakage & juncture.
Once more I enter a still life of my making, living
   the strangest of lives, a prisoner free to come & go.
Each thing I touch with a story that lives as long
   as I live. But no longer.
Days lived once & forever in this room.
This room that will one day be emptied by hands
   not my own.

Stonington, 8 A.M.

ELIZABETH SPIRES

She went back to the island after twenty years
to find it hadn't changed. But she herself had changed.
She struggled against nostalgia, a rosy lens
tinting the grey-shingled houses running up the hill,
the grey-shingled shacks perched at water's edge,
a greyish-rose, everything luminous, slightly aglow.

A Sunday sun if ever there was one illuminated
St. Mary Star of the Sea, perched on the highest hill,
its bell ringing madly, "Come in! Come in!"
Everything was just the way she remembered:
the Opera House, lettered on its harbor side
in giant capital letters, OPERA HOUSE,
the little grocery store, post office, granite museum,
one-room library, marine supply, B&B, and town café,
even the ramshackle, peeling dockside shop
where the same gray man in the same gray cardigan
sold postcards, newspapers, and souvenirs.
Was this a place where no one ever died?

The tide was going out. Gulls waded in shallows,

crying "Hey! Ha!" to no one, sounding so human.

Trying to capture it all, a Sunday painter

in a broad-brimmed hat and low rubber boots

had confidently set up her easel in the muck.

Above, a three-quarter moon hung

like a smudged thumbprint, soon to disappear.

All of it, in its own way, a perfect composition,

until a boat coming in from Isle au Haut cut swiftly

across the scene, slashing a watery diagonal

into the picture to make a completely different picture.

Ice

PETER BEHRENS

SOON AFTER I MET YOU WE TOOK A TRIP. I had an appetite
for mileage, for geography, and I persuaded you to leave town
with me because I wanted to see what would happen. I was
moving fast and you let yourself be carried along. I remember
riding across a prairie landscape in eastern Washington, on an
afternoon between storms, and driving over a pass with ghostly
elk on the highway. We slept in a Chinese motel in Vancou-
ver, crossed the Strait, traversed the Island, rented the smallest
of cabins on a beach miles from anywhere. It was late November, rainy, fog bound, the off-season. By then I needed you to
fall in love with me. And I had to walk out every second evening to place long distance calls to a woman waiting for me in
Toronto. You knew about her but I don't remember us talking about her. Instead we walked on the beach where the fog
smelled of cedar smoke, and scavengers who lived in pearl-grey
shacks helped themselves to lumber that drifted in, washed and
polished by the tide.

We slept together and remained strangers, sometimes taking our walks alone. You needed time to think, you needed privacy. I wanted to stay on that beach with you forever.

As soon as we drove back into the mountains the rain
changed to snow. At certain times the highway was closed and
I remember motel rooms with you. I needed to savor the miles
we had left and use them sparingly because you were nearly
mine while we were travelling, you almost belonged to me.

Long before dark I would start scanning the outskirts of towns for motels, even when you insisted that you were prepared to drive all night, or at least another hundred miles, or just over the next pass, to the next town.

"Too dangerous," I'd say. "Too slippery." I was worried about black ice, worried about losing you. I was grateful for the storms because I wanted to keep travelling in your company, and if the weather had been clear we would have reached our town in a day and a half instead of the four days it took us finally. I relished the small rooms, the polyester sheets, each rented bed you shared with me.

In the middle of a storm, somewhere in the Bitterroots, we stopped beside a broken guard rail where the air was crowded with falling snow and black, greasy smoke. We rolled down our windows, heard flames snapping. The afternoon smelled of roasting meat. We got out of the car, walked to the edge of the road and peered down at a *Swift's Sausage & Premium Hams* eighteen-wheeler sprawled like a stunned animal at the bottom of a gully. Snow was falling thickly; it was a curtain blocking everything except subdued orange flames licking the sides of the trailer. Snow sizzled on blackened metal.

We started slipping down the bank. I jumped up on the running board and peered inside, expecting to see the driver's body; but he had already been taken away. Snow blew through the broken windows and rattled crisply along the vinyl dashboard. Crumbs of safety glass were scattered over the seat and the rubber floor. A pair of elk-hide gloves, stiff and sweat-stained, were wedged above the big sun visor.

Standing on the running board, gripping the big truck mirror, I looked around and saw you falling backwards, laughing, flapping your arms and making an angel in the snow, and I recognized with a kind of gasping, breathtaking, pain how much had changed in ten days, how you were ruining my past, making it dim and unimportant, how I was living for nothing except you, the road, the snow, the invisible mountains.

I looked up the embankment, to my car—engine idling, doors flung open, tail lights shining through falling grey snow. It seemed extraordinarily beautiful; hopeful; a promise of everything to come.

Trips taken by lovers who don't know each other very well can have unforeseen consequences. Attachment itself is a mystery.

At some point I told you I was prepared to push everything as far as it would go. *Hope, faith,* and *passion* were talismanic words to me then but when I said them to you they only seemed to drive you in on yourself, you became quieter.

When we arrived back in town the weather was inhospitably cold, the river had seized and hunks of ice were locked beneath the bridge. It was the middle of the morning and we ate breakfast in the cafe. The town was stunned under snowdrifts, our friends had vanished. We went back to my room.

I was in love, you were wary, and the inequity felt hot, something I could never swallow or digest. I kept telling you to trust me. I studied road maps while you slept. When you woke I suggested California, Mexico. You didn't believe I was serious. I told myself when the time was ripe I'd convince you. I went out to make a call to Toronto. I had promised to return there by Christmas. She wanted to know exactly when I would be arriving. She knew me better than you did, though I was always lying to her, always trying to give the truth to you. She sounded anxious and I fended her off with impatient lies.

We stayed in my room for most of a week. It kept snowing, a foot of snow a day, and I believed I was winning you. To be precise, I thought that you were getting weaker, that before long you'd be going anywhere with me.

Overnight, Arctic air blew the sky clear. You said you needed to get out for a few hours, no matter how cold it was. We rented skis and drove a few miles out of town, my car rattling over the road on frozen tires and stiffened springs. Snow in the woods lay deep and untracked which was why we decided to travel across the lake. The air rasped our throats and lungs. Limestone mountains glittered around the shore.

Years later I told our story to my wife after she and I had only known each other for a couple of hours. We were sitting in darkness on a beach on Cape Cod. "I heard her scream," I said, "then I looked down and saw the snow around my skis turning blue. When I looked back she was falling."

The beach was on approximately the same latitude as Portugal. It was midnight and we had been swimming in the white surf. She had slipped out of her clothes and dived in. It wasn't very dangerous in the waves but there was a slight rip-tide, an element of treachery.

I think I told her the story because I wanted her to believe that I was capable of loving someone. If she had interrupted at any point to ask what it really was about I would have said, *passion*. For a long time I have been trying to attach an acceptable meaning to our story.

You slipped into the water wearing skis as narrow as bones strapped to your feet. As I lay down for you the ice beneath my belly began to soften. I held out something to you, a stick or a ski pole, but it was ignored, and then the ice below my body began to crumble. The cold water struck my chest like the flat blade of a shovel swung hard. I could feel my lungs shriveling.

We bobbed in the hole while our lips were being sealed. I kept ducking beneath the surface, trying to detach my skis. The water in my eyes was black and burning. Breathing was difficult and noisy. When I tried to launch myself out of the hole, every piece of ice I touched crumbled in my hands. After a while it seemed less than sensible to struggle. Your breathing sounded like an engine with something severely wrong. Your hair was laced with white frost, your face was lumpy and pale, you kept looking surprised. Still we kicked, sputtered and splashed, trying to keep apart so our skis wouldn't tangle. I already felt sorry for your family. The rest of my thinking was being lulled as the cold settled in. Water slopped back and forth, subsided, and a skin of soft, new ice began forming at the rim of the hole. We would look at each other then look away. Dying together was a little humiliating.

I told our story to another woman. We were sitting in a booth in the Chinese cafe last week. When I finished, she reminded me that J. Edgar Hoover kept boxes and cardboard cartons sealed with masking tape in his basement and the back of his garage. Inside were his *raw files*, which he used to guard and extend his power.

"Are these your raw files?" she said.

I told her you and I had often sat in that same booth. I pointed out items on the menu that you used to order. She said, "You have the structure of a story all set up and now you're trying to fit me into it."

She said, "Where is your wife?"

A piece of ice held and I was kicking, slowly at first, not much caring. Then with a little more will. Did you even notice? I surprised myself when I flopped up on the ice and stuck to it, sucking and gasping. All my clothes became hard, instantly. You drifted nearby, I touched the collar of your jacket, or it could have been one of your braids. Was your hat off by then? You came out on your own, pushing and kicking. You had abandoned your boots and skis in the water. You lay on the ice making sounds.

We began crawling. The trees on the shore grew bigger, then stopped, and after a while we realized we were no longer crawling toward them. Instead we were pretending to sleep. I got up and started running and you came after me. We moved like monsters in our stiff clothes, lurching and grunting. When we reached the shore I broke off my icy hunks of skis. We were taking air in sore gasps. I started through the snowdrifts and you followed, shouting in pain because your feet were so tender.

We couldn't see the car for a long time but then it appeared. The key was in the zippered pocket of your jacket. Neither of us could grasp the zipper so I pulled the jacket off you, hooked it on the bumper, and tore the pocket open. The key dropped onto the snow. It took a long time to pick it up—it was so smooth, cold, and slender. Finally we got the door open.

I was trying to start the engine when another car chugged over the bridge. These people seemed to know what to do. They got us into their car and began driving to the hospital. I sat in the front seat and a woman tore my clothes open with a knife, pulled off her shirt, pressed her hot breasts against me. I could hear you in the back seat, suffering. The car floated into the town. At the hospital they went to work on me first and left you in the hallway in a puddle of water on the floor.

Six hours later we were released and went back to my room wearing borrowed clothes.

I called Toronto twice while heading east that Christmas. From a café in South Dakota; a motel in Michigan.

By the time I arrived, she knew something was wrong. She said she had known for a long time how things would end. She was angry with me for driving all that way to tell her I was in love with someone else. The next year she met another man and married wisely, flowering with conjugal zeal. I see her whenever I'm in her city. There isn't much to say, yet I feel compelled. She would rather I didn't need to see her but she is gracious. And I don't stay very long. A single cup of tea and I am on my way, following subway maps through the city of Toronto.

You and I had a short subsequent history. It's not important what went wrong, is it? The flaws of character and circumstance that kept us apart? I could list most of them and it would be depressing, but it wouldn't matter.

Is our story about *passion, faithlessness,* or is it about an accident, a series of accidents? What seems important now is how much I remember. Your kiss in a supermarket parking lot. An argument in a basement apartment. You turning away from me, at an airport, while engines roared.

In the middle of that night, you woke up howling. Your skin was on fire, you felt it broiling and burning and sloughing off your bones. I led you into the bathroom, shut the door, turned on the hot water. It roared from the tap and the bathroom packed with steam. Your hair was damp and fragrant, your body shone in the fogged mirror, your skin was the color of light.

"Ice" first appeared in *Saturday Night* (Toronto).

AN EXCHANGE

About things and other things

GREGORY MAGUIRE AND ANN PATCHETT

August 8, 2018
Gregory Maguire to Ann Patchett

Dear Ann,

Do you remember I wrote you last year about my New Year's resolution—not last January's, but the prior one? 18 months ago or more? This because you had written an essay about some kind of exercise in avoiding the thing-iness of things? Was it about monitoring your *getting and spending*? In any case, our separate instincts seemed to have a family feeling, somehow.

I told you I was going to get rid of three things a day for a year. Goodwill, largely. But library sales, too, and trash bins, and gifts to friends, and junk at the curb.

I realize you've never visited me in my home, so you'll have to trust me when I say I am neither a hoarder nor am I a slob. Rather, I'm ferociously organized and industrious. Also clean and a neatnik though not clinically antiseptic about it. I prefer a nice sandalwood candle to Lysol in the downstairs loo.

500-odd days later, I'm still at this dread campaign. I count individual books separately, but if I give away a clutch of notecards with their envelopes, I count that clutch as one item. If I throw out a pair of socks, it counts as one item, not two socks.

Also I'm honorable. Throwing out limp celery from the crisper doesn't count. Neither do old light bulbs nor cardboard tubes from paper towels count.

My problem is that after 18 months, some 1650 items and rising, I am still the only one who notices any difference in the house. It looks and feels the same not only to guests but to all the other members of the family.

I think I need a reminder about what your resolution was. And maybe an update as to how it's going?

I'm heading for the airport tomorrow night—off to London the next morning—but I find this question continues to intrigue me. Maybe it's the ordeal of packing.

X Gregory

Aug. 8, 2018
Ann Patchett to Gregory Maguire

What's interesting to me about this is that I think we may be cut from the same bolt of cloth. I have a neat home and cleaning is how I soothe myself. If I have to figure out a tough problem in my novel, I clean the oven. So I get how, while it might look like getting rid of three things a day is a sacrifice, it is in fact a joy. I haven't tried getting rid of three things a day but I get rid of a LOT of stuff. I picture myself sitting at my desk looking around and thinking, okay, who's next? A few days ago I gave away a piggy bank that I had bought at an auction two years ago. Laura Castillo had decorated it and I really loved it, but the Book Industry Charitable Foundation people were having another auction and I thought, okay, I've enjoyed this pig for two years. Shouldn't I send it back out to make more money? I've been trying to experiment with giving away things I love instead of just getting rid of the stuff I don't use. Having a bookstore is very helpful in this regard, as I now feel I have twenty daughters of all ages and sizes. I'll bring in a beautiful blouse, an admired pair of shoes, and they go nuts. It's very gratifying.

My experiment was to stop buying things and yours was to get rid of what you already have, and in both cases I think it becomes a sort of self-soothing act, like cleaning. How do we organize the enormous amount of really lovely stuff we own? And how do we crawl out from beneath the weight of it all? Last year I threw out every plaque and award. "Southeastern Booksellers Best Novel of the Year, 1998." That shit stacks up. I look at my belongings and think, Okay, if I'm dead will anybody want this or will it just be a burden to someone? That exercise gives a lot of guidance.

Tell me about your parents. Are they alive? Have you had to downsize them? My father died three and a half years ago. I've cleaned out his garage, his file cabinets. He and my stepmother traveled all over the world and he saved everything, the menus from ships, the postcards. I can take fifty color pictures of my father in New Zealand and throw them in the trash because who will want them when I'm dead? My mother is 81 and lives three blocks away from me. I've downsized her twice and the battles between us were epic. She had 120 wine glasses when I moved her last. She doesn't have parties but she imagines she'll have parties. It was excruciating, but also very informative about how I want to live my life.

Over to you. Why and where are you going for a month?

X Ann

Aug. 9, 2018
Gregory Maguire to Ann Patchett

Well, you've *got it in one*, as the British say. My scheme of perpetual-deaccession became formalized after the death of my remaining parent.

My stepmother, who raised me since I was about 2, passed

away five years ago at the age of 95. Fully compos mentis until near the actual end, she lived alone in her own home until the final four months, when my younger sister moved in to help. The house was a 1905 American foursquare in a streetcar suburb, as they called them back then. Stand-alone wooden houses without driveways, some villa-style, others less gussied up. Ours was a midrange 9-room home with two bathrooms, a full attic and basement. My folks bought it at a distress sale after the previous owner's misadventures with the Internal Revenue Service.

As co-executor, I was charged with clearing out the house. Marie had lived so long that none of her seven children now needed anything from our childhood home but mementos and tokens. But however neatly arranged, the sheer *stuff* of a life! The stuff of nine lives lived between those walls, really. Not only every cancelled check she'd ever written, every paid bill and every tax return from 1955 through 2012. Not just every letter ever received since her wedding day. Not only all 3,500 clipped columns, on that gently tattering newsprint that colors into buttercream and then into mocha the farther down in the pile they go, columns that my dad had written for the local paper over a 17-year period. No, it was also approximately 60 half-used sets of paper napkins from a half-century's worth of family celebrations. Dozens of vases that bouquets had come in. Hundreds of unused greeting cards. Thousands of books. Three floors of shabby beloved furniture (and not a stick of it beautiful or valuable).

In the end, yes, we did hire a skip and throw out a load and a half of junk. But not until I'd spent months trying to place things, like unused skeins of acrylic yarn in church groups making blankets for refugees. I harried the usual suspects: the Salvation Army, the local preschools, the soup kitchens in the city. ("Do you need a few ladles? Yes, they're old, but hardly rusty at all, and they don't have any holes in them.")

I came away, at last, realizing that my mother's robust physical and intellectual strengths and her fiscal smarts, honed in Depression Era–poverty, served her until the very end. They meant she had never had to downsize. The job left to us, therefore, was the more onerous because it had never even been begun.

She wasn't a hoarder. Nor, as I said earlier, am I. But I realized that everything I have doesn't have to be held to be cherished. And if I give it away and I forget about it and never think about it again, how much of a loss is that, really?

It's my kids and my husband I think about, and the terrible job I'd leave them if at least I don't try to beat back the rubble as it multiplies during my lifetime.

On the matter of pigs and piggy banks, I'll only say this. I was asked to paint one or two for auction items recently. A benefit for booksellers, wasn't it? Hoping to appeal to someone who hasn't been afflicted with an aversion to possessions, I painted two porcelain piggy banks, one of Glinda the Good Witch and one of Elphaba the Wicked Witch of the West. As pigs they don't look Broadway-ready, though they could oink their way into a picture book, maybe. I added for each of them a little testimonial poem to be inserted in the money slot. The credo for the one called Elphabank went like this:

I keep here only what I need.
I do not need a lot.
What I don't need I give away.
I don't save for a rainy day.
(I'm not much for a rainy day.
It tends to make me melt away.)
To save a little isn't greed.
To save a lot is greed indeed.
To give a lot is not.

It's a bit smarmy and self-satisfied, like the character. I hope someone pays buckets for it and benefits booksellers the nation over.

Enough of this—I really have to finish packing. You asked where I'm going. I'm taking my younger kids to London on Saturday, and then we catch the Eurostar to Avignon. If we have to haul our own luggage, it cuts down on the number of souvenirs we're all tempted to buy.

But I leave you with wild curiosity about this question of streamlining—unloading—restricting purchases—the physical stuff of life—and its possible symbolic resemblance to the notion of the crafting of fictions. "How do we crawl from beneath the weight of it all?" you ask. Isn't that like the dread one feels at the start of a novel? When virtually anything really CAN happen, and might—and the act of creation is partly the act of jettisoning the attractive nuisances that occur to one's plot-addicted creative brain?

X Gregory

Aug. 11, 2018
Ann Patchett to Gregory Maguire

Oh, Gregory, isn't it all about death, by which I mean absolutely everything? Without the life to animate the objects, the objects are all so sad. When my beloved grandmother died she had a single closet that took up the floor space of six shoe boxes in two lines. She had a small chest of drawers and a bedside table and bookshelf. Period. I can sit here at my desk and put my eyes on a little porcelain flower basket and a small yellow pitcher in the shape of a jay hawk that she kept pencils in on her desk. I also have her little manual typewriter that types in cursive.

That Philip Larkin poem comes to mind always, "Home Is So Sad." My brother-in-law died with about that much stuff four years ago. When I cleaned out his closet all of his shoes had holes in them. Two months ago my second stepfather died and I emptied his room in assisted living by myself in two hours. So there's the terrible scenario that is your stepmother (oh, how heartbreaking it is to think of you trying to find good homes for those ladles!), and the equally sad and utterly different scenario of my stepfather. The trick, of course, is to find people who are tender enough to want the stuff. My sister has a big soft heart and took so many things that belonged to our dad, all the little painted lead soldiers he collected over the years. I'll have nothing to do with it. Fortunately, I come from a long line of poor people on both sides so there are no heirlooms to protect. If I can remember when something was purchased, I owe it no allegiance.

Why did I stop buying things? Why are you giving things away? Because those things are *sad*, because you realize at some point the Buddhists were right and the things we buy as talismans to distract us from thoughts of our own suffering and death will, at some point, start reminding us of suffering and death. People are always complaining that movies and television are pitched to the young, but they're the only ones who haven't caught on. They still want to spend money because they haven't realized they're going to die. All advertising should be for them.

I have an 86-year-old nun I take care of, Sister Nena. Nena and her nun cohorts really turned out to be the big winners at the end because the vow of poverty (which gets a little loose in later years) is in fact freedom. Nena loves to say to me, "It's just *stuff*," as in, the shiny things that are meant to distract us from God or death or whatever you want to call it.

My dread at the start of a novel is "How do I get in?" I can see the house, and I circle and circle but don't know how I'll ever break inside.

Do you ever worry that writing a novel is just another way of hiding? That's my fear.

I watched an Oprah video of you and Andy and the kids the other day. Do you still have three? Do they want a lot of things? This is such a perverse thing to say but I think it would be hard to have a lot of money and children. How do you control your desire to give them everything, thus distracting them from thoughts of suffering and death?

Are you sorry you got into this with me?

And where are you now?

X Ann

Aug. 18, 2018
Gregory Maguire to Ann Patchett

So much—we started with a single strand and now have about six running.

A metaphor for how we accumulate so quickly. . . .?

But people who write letters rather than texts have to save up the running storylines. Are novelists the last people to write actual letters? Don't answer that—it's just another diversion.

Yes, the line of enquiry is ultimately about death, I suppose. All of it—writing novels and trying to shrug off the excess impedimenta (I understand that word is the Latin for "luggage," or "baggage," and doesn't that just fit?) Also about death: the having of children. And the writing of novels.

I asked my brother Matt (one of my six siblings) if he still would agree to be my executor, with my husband Andy, when I die. He snorted on the phone line. "We were co-executors of our mother's estate, and you did 96 percent of the work," he reminded me. (He's right, but it was more like 98 percent.) "Do you really trust me to handle your affairs?"

Well, no. But that's why I'm doing what of it I can before I get anywhere near ill or old enough not to manage. It's not to preserve a mausoleum of my own precious stuff, my own teenage angsty words. It's to save any of my heirs and assigns (husband, kids, brother Matt) to have to spend any extra half hour of *their* precious lives thinking "Would Gregory/Ba/Greg have wanted this to be saved? And what should we do with it?"

I'm trying to make all those choices myself—archives, manuscripts, etc.—so it is just a matter of someone putting my intentions into effect, wrapping it up in a few hours, with time left over to go get a pint or two at close of business. I'm busy transcribing 45 years of journals. I'm not sure exactly why, except perhaps to keep anyone else from ever having to decide whether to do all that work or not.

One of John Updike's quotes about writing: what was it? Oh, from one of his poems in *Endpoint*. Wow, this is a lot of what we're talking about. Here's eight lines from the middle of it.

> Here in this place of arid clarity,
> two thousand miles from where my souvenirs
> collect a cozy dust, the piled produce
> of bald ambition pulling ignorance,
> I see clear through to the ultimate page,
> the silence I dared break for my small time.
> No piece was easy, but each fell finished,
> in its shroud of print, into a book-shaped hole.

That book-shaped hole is the grave into which every book, even *The Da Vinci Code*, eventually falls. We don't write for immortality. We write for mortality itself.

And to finish on this note, a quote from Jill Paton Walsh, English novelist and dear friend, the last line from her Library of Congress speech, "The Lords of Time." Nearly verbatim (I don't have it beside me): "Nothing that we value will endure in the world unless the young can be freely persuaded to cherish it too."

The gelignitic word there is "freely."

Where are we? In France, breasting "le canicule"—the dog days of summer. Fans on in every room, not quite drowning out the torrents of Aretha Franklin we are playing in memoriam. Now there's a legacy it'll be hard to quiet.

As to having kids, writing books—running bookstores—the labor itself is the reward. As in Cavafy's "Ithaka"—the getting there is the point, not the having arrived.

And all the questions you raise about the problems we have with impedimenta apply to my kids, too. One child is a gourmand and an aesthete and eschews anything less than top drawer; one is a natural ascetic; and one a hoarder-in-training-wheels. (Though all adopted, they all take after me.) I guess we've covered the waterfront.

Which waterfront? No, not the Côte d'Azur. We're in what I call "budget Provence"—the department of Le Garde, known as one of the poorer districts of the south. A little too dry to have attracted painters, and thus relatively free of tourists. No one in our village speaks English. This turns me monastic as I speak nearly no French. Another useful moment, learning to husband words. It's about time I started, after 45 years of journal writing.

(Do you know of the Cape Cod writer who has taken a vow of silence and one day a week doesn't speak at all? If she has to go out, she carries a card with her that explains her campaign. It's another strategy of continence, of Zen discipline. Custody of the senses. It might be easy to do this as an author, but it wouldn't be so easy to carry off as a parent or as a bookstore owner.)

X Gregory

Aug 20, 2018
Ann Patchett to Gregory Maguire

Impedimenta! Wouldn't that be a fantastic name for a llama? I'm very impressed with your work on your journals but I won't be following your lead. I plan to pitch mine in the fireplace, and not because I'm private but because the journals are unspeakably tedious. I write down the events of the day with maybe half a sentence for my emotional state. I do it religiously (I do *everything* religiously) to make a map of where I've been. They were very helpful when I was writing *Truth & Beauty* because I knew when I'd been with Lucy, when she had surgery, when she tried to kill herself. I looked at the one for this year to check on something about my novel and was horrified by all that's happened—my mother's hip replacement, two stepfathers dying. The journals prove that time supplies a narrative, even if you can't see it on any given day.

This from a recent email from my editor: "My sister died a month ago after a long and grueling decline, and I had to travel to Mexico to clear up her estate, such as it was. Sad work. There's such poignancy about the things people leave behind." That is the long and the short of it: the reason not to shop, the reason to give things away, the reason to act responsibly in relationship to *things*. I wish to create as little poignancy as possible. But then of course there's the poignancy of my grandmother and brother-in-law and their two boxes of worldly possessions. It's a kinder sort of sadness.

There's a memoir out that I've heard is great called *They Left Us Everything*. I think the situation would be comparable to your stepmother.

Is there a vanity in thinking that we're going to impact death, shape the experience of our death for others? I wonder. No. It IS a kindness to get rid of things. I'm sure of it.

Why did I think Updike was a bad poet? When he was alive I thought *The New Yorker* indulged him by publishing his poems and now every time I read one I think they're fantastic. Sigh. Oh, Updike.

I just spent three weeks in Utah not speaking (save the nightly phone call home) and I am still feeling the benefits of this massive realignment. I was built for silence and solitude, as so many of us were. The entire trip felt like a meditation. And here was my major revelation: that I had to stop anticipating the needs of others. I could meet the needs of others, but I needed to stop putting energy into trying to foresee the need and meet it before it had ever been felt by the other person, that not only was it a waste of time, it was a downright irritating thing to do.

Karl, my husband, just bought a plane. He'll be 71 in November. He's had many planes in the past but he hasn't had one for the last 15 years. After talking about this nonstop for five years, he put down the deposit last week. We could easily start another thread about how it feels to think of your beloved who just had double cataract surgery flying around in a single-engine Cirrus, but let's table that for now. I had LOADS of time to soul-search on this one and came to the conclusions that 1) I can't keep him safe. 2) If this is a source of joy for him and we've got the money, he should have what he wants. So here's my question for you: is there anything you want? As in, a thing you want for yourself? There are plenty of things I want to do for other people and for charities (Book Industry Charitable Foundation—BINC!) but I can't think of any THING I want to have. That makes Karl's desire to own a plane sort of touching. I mean, he's still capable of that kind of a want. When I was in Utah and went to the grocery store alone to feed only myself I realized I didn't even know what I ate. What food do I like if I'm all alone? Is it that I've reached a higher spiritual plane or am I some sort of service animal?

Discuss!

Love, Ann (I'm making the jump as I find that the outcome of this exchange is that I am loving you.)

Aug 20, 2018
Gregory Maguire to Ann Patchett

Likewise! And I haven't even allowed myself the temptation to write to you about nuns. (My Concord Free Press novel, *The Next Queen of Heaven*, is full of nuns like your Sister Nena. A journalist once asked me why I have written so often about witches; my answer, meant to elicit a laugh, was "Because I went to Catholic schools and was taught by nuns." But of course every joke carries its coiled, clandestine truth, and I realized later that I meant "taught by women who were brave, smart, self-effacing; and in having given everything else up that society cherishes, tells us to lust after, were freer than the rest of us in the ways that the spirit—including the artist's spirit— yearns for.")

And of course, everyone looks smart in black, esp. witches and old-style nuns. (One of whom is partly responsible for my becoming a writer.)

But I will write more again soon. I have to take two of my kids to procure more junk in the local rialto, called the Inter- marché.

Love, too.
Gregory

Aug 21, 2018
Ann Patchett to Gregory Maguire

Nuns! Wait, should we really stop without a discussion of the spiritual freedom that comes from submission? What about the fact that we were both raised under the thrall of women who made poverty look so good?

I bought Sister Nena a little house and keep her up. She is 86. She is my religion.

Love and goodnight.

Aug. 21, 2018
Gregory Maguire to Ann Patchett

I'm getting sad already because I can feel we're about to take a break from this. I have guests coming in a couple of days from Greece and managing a village house in France with kids and guests, and further travel looming the following week, will break my concentration.

But I feel as if we've been on a midnight bus ride and we started talking in, say, Syracuse, at midnight, and we're nearing Terre Haute, Indiana, and we've only paused our discussion now and then at a rest stop.

For me, the examination of conscience moment approaches. (It's a habit from childhood that I still practice if only for a few seconds at a time.) We've been talking about lightening our load, using two different strategies—me by shucking things, you by resisting the temptation to accumulate. The sine qua non is that we both know we're lucky and privileged to bother with such concerns. It's a luxury to choose to trim—it implies surfeit.

We've also, then, below the surface, been talking about greed—I'll limit myself to the singular possessive, and say *mine mine mine*—I won't presume that for you. Greed for a few beautiful things—even greed for fewer beautiful things. It's a sybarite's folly on my part. But we're part of a national culture and an increasingly monolithic global culture, and the mighty furnace that powers monolithia is greed, I fear. (I distinguish between greed and need, both here and in my book *Egg & Spoon*.) You have distinguished between them, too, not prohibiting yourself from buying Windex and Motrin and paper for your printer. I read that in your *New York Times* piece about your experiment.

Once out of college, I spent two years considering the priesthood. I visited seminaries. (I had worked my way through college as a choirmaster, and I was in love with *The Sound of*

Music, but never mind about that.) As a spiritual exercise in simplicity I limited my wardrobe to nothing but clean blue jeans and white shirts. To be honest, I was aware that I looked my limited best in that garb, at that age. But more to the point, daily I rescued for myself some five to ten minutes a morning I'd have otherwise spent trying to figure out what to wear. Ten more minutes of life each day that I could spend more fruitfully than on my wardrobe. To read poetry daily—which I did. To pray (sometimes). To write letters. This was a habit I took up, a habit I was trying on.

At the advice of a young and vital priest friend, who said I would be crushed in the institution of the priesthood, I turned away from that. Instead, I chose to write and teach, to adopt kids with my boyfriend and then to marry him when it became legal. But there is still a cord of yearning in me for the idiorhythmic hermitage— some recurring appetite for less, rather than more.

Here are a few things I want to remember to share before we get off the bus. (I see there are about a dozen questions you asked I didn't answer. And your husband in an airplane? I would die if my husband even proposed it, and that would solve all my problems at once.) My last hurried thoughts are both about writing and about this weird exercise of dispossession, if you will.

One of the quotes on my family wall (photos of my relatives and friends and quotes from my spiritual, writer friends) is from E. M Forster. "My defense at any Last Judgment would be *I was trying to connect up and use all the fragments I was born with.*"

For me that is what writing is—once a passion is committed to story, it is given away. The writer is liberated from that obsession. Lighter, freer. (Also, perhaps, more open for further grace of inspiration?)

Another one is putatively from da Vinci; I think I saw this

carved in an entablature in Amboise, where he died. "He who possesses most must be most afraid of loss."

And upon the tombstone of Nikos Kazantzakis, who, having been excommunicated, was buried outside the consecrated ground of Heraklion, Crete, is written: "I hope for nothing. I fear nothing. I am free."

While we're alive, we can't avoid hoping and fearing, and we can't achieve freedom. But I guess the act of trying, one way or another, is an okay way of living.

They're announcing the terminus approaching. What can you tell me while there is still time?

Aug. 21, 2018
Ann Patchett to Gregory Maguire

"I hope for nothing. I fear nothing. I am free." That's where the conversation ends. Beautiful. Thank you for that, and for all of this. It's been such a privilege to think with you.

I sometimes wonder how people who don't write books survive the weight of having to carry their lives around with them. I can struggle in a book and leave the struggle there. I can leave so many details of my life in books. Lucy Grealy pressed into a book like a leaf. I'm so lucky for that.

If there were endless time we'd talk more about Catholicism. I would wonder to what point someone without our past would even want to enter into this conversation. I am still wearing gray-pleated skirts and white blouses. I still, in my heart of hearts, believe that poverty is the highest calling, and I am ashamed that I am not brave enough to give up everything (or nearly everything) to truly help the poor with what I have. That is so deep in me. I know the right thing to do and I don't do it. And maybe it's enough that I'll do it when I'm dead, though then of course I'm dead and won't enjoy it.

There isn't a beautiful thing I want, or if I want it, I just sit with it for a minute and the feeling passes. It always cracks me up, those moments I still think I want another necklace. But greed, sure, I've got plenty of greed, it's just for time and love and attention and probably fame though I'm loath to admit it.

We haven't talked about charity. We haven't talked about the Four Noble Truths. But there's the bus station in the distance. And your company is coming. And my novel is so nearly finished.

We'll keep in touch, won't we?

Love, Ann

Lina

MADISON SMARTT BELL

IN REACH OF HIS DESIRE AT LAST; her alabaster body within his compass, the touch of his two hands. His curved palms tingled, burned almost. Did that extraordinary heat rise shimmering from her whiteness? The translucent pallor that had always drawn him to her face and forearms had, till now, always seemed rather cool and distant, a quality which was part of the attraction (he knew that from the start). Sweet Lina, composed of honey and milk, at last prepared to surrender her sweetness, and surely he was swollen, taut with desire.

Curious, the sofa on which she half-reclined, the bed clothes lowered to her hips, so his stinging eyes swam over her bare navel and the white round breasts that seemed to look toward him, while her head in fact was turned away—somehow in disarmed modesty? But surely not; Lina had never been abashed. Yet now, when he had done her will, when she must yield herself to what he had for so long wished, perhaps she was. It was a sort of chaise longue, really, where she had arranged herself, one hand caught up behind her head (supporting a more elaborate coiffure than Lina usually affected) with its back scrolled like the stern of a sleigh, and there seemed hardly room on it for one, though doubtless they would sort that out, one way or another. Doubt: he had never seen any such piece of furniture in Lina's place, and why had she got herself up in this, well, archaic manner?

To commemorate their union, maybe. Lina had always her sense of ceremony, of occasion, though it had not often worked to his advantage. In a flash he saw that turning her head aside like that was her way of offering her white throat, the *V* of alabaster muscle revealed there.

He closed his burning mouth against it, with a sigh that swelled to a moan. The crystalline sweetness of her was there at the tip of his tongue. At the moment he grasped her white shoulders they crumbled into glittering, acrid powder, burning his nostrils and blinding him; his hands were empty of anything now and he no longer knew where she was.

... where he was. The face seemed printed on the inside of the shroud that covered him. Rather a pretty, charming face, possibly a little impish, and rendered with just a few sprinkling gestures, like cinnamon sprinkled over the surface of *café au lait*. Curling hair, faintly slanted eyes, perk of nose and the hint of a smile. Two or three things I know about her.

Angel in my coffee cup. Like the visage of Jesus baked into a bagel. A groaning sound filled the space around him... rush of wind crying over a bottle. His vision pulled back, like a camera on a dolly. He was here—where? He knew he didn't want to know.

Movement of muscle under the skin animated the cinnamon face, which floated toward him now, again, till it encompassed all he saw.

First real kisses are so strange. She seemed to be saying it somewhere down inside his blood, while they were still inside the kiss... a deep one. His heart swelled—a physical effect, not an emotion. Now he could see her mouth, shaping the words dreamily, blurred with a lipstick so dark a red it was almost black. Centered in the ice-pallor of her face, *so strange.* He had a sudden impression that she had taken something out of him when she pulled up and away from the kiss. Impossible she should have swallowed his heart.

They were on a balcony, or in a stairwell—in any case both leaning on some balustrade or railing. His hand slipped under the rail and grasped a bar. There other people down below them—from the same party, he thought. He thought they were attending a party. If not for the drug he would have been almost too drunk. If not for her he wouldn't have taken it. Never something he had much cared for, but he wanted to share with her something she liked. Because seldom in his life had he said *no*.

When he reached for Lina again she moved away.

The blood-drunk sensation of Lina. Paul had met her in the way of ordinary business. He worked as a masseur sometimes. He made house-calls. Paul's friend Shelly had given Lina his number. Both women worked in small-time theater; Shelly as a manager, Lina as an actress. Lina had, according to Shelly, injured her shoulder in some onstage stunt. She knew Paul was good with that sort of thing.

Lina's apartment was in the East Village, a long way out 13th Street, a no-go area when Paul had first moved to the city, a long time before. Whole blocks of it had been an open heroin market back in the day. Now he strolled comfortably, carrying his folded table like an outsized briefcase, looking at the gentrified restaurants and boutiques with a sort of Rip-Van-Winkle bemusement.

A fourth floor walk-up. It was a little awkward jacking the table around the corners of the staircase, but Paul was used to that kind of difficulty. The steps themselves were splintered, worn to a bow shape in the middle. The landings were tiled in the tight diamond pattern used in all such tenements long ago.

"It's open." Lina's voice, muffled by the door. Paul hesitated, then turned the knob. The door swung into the kitchen, where the enormous old bathtub was too—nicely refurbished, its claw feet even gilded.

Lina stood up from her bath and captured Paul's eyes so completely with her own that he didn't look at her body at all, though somehow he was still aware of the pert turn of her breasts, the trickles of clear water running down from her navel through the puff of golden hair between her legs. Her eyes were the green of a dreaming cat's.

He could hear birds, nearer than the open window in the room behind the kitchen. A goldfinch flew to perch on Lina's extended finger. Paul had run into all sorts of florid behavior from his massage clients, but at this point he became reasonably certain that he must be hallucinating.

Lina appeared to blush, though ever so slightly, no more than the faintest tint of peach. She flicked her finger and the bird took flight, dipping under the lintel of the door to the other room.

"Oh," said Lina. "Could you hand me the towel?" Both her right arm and her right nipple turned to point to the thing she wanted. Her voice was surprisingly deep, with a richer timbre than he had been able to hear on the phone.

Paul set up his table in the other room. Lina slept here, he could tell, from the futon unfurled in an alcove, but one would hardly have called it a bedroom. There was a desk and chair and a window-seat, and Lina's headshots were tacked up all about, often veiled with colored translucent scarves, and interspersed with fine art posters: Fuselli's "Nightmare" and another 16th-century work of the school of Fontainebleu, depicting two gentlewomen nude from the waist up in their bath, looking out at the viewer with calm contempt. There were a lot of finches fluttering about, and twittering. With a slight start, Paul noticed that behind two Plexiglass doors under the window seat were snakes, plenty of them, mostly colorfully striped boas, but one, a large one, a solid mustardy yellow.

He covered the massage table with a plain white sheet.

"They're harmless," Lina said, as she flung herself forward onto the platform. She'd changed the towel for a flowered cotton kimono. The damp rounds of her body had still wet it through. Paul flashed on the image of her rising from the tub; apparently he'd seen and retained more than he'd thought.

"How do you want me?" Lina rolled to one side, opening her leg and raising her foot to the ceiling, turning her head to admire her own flexibility. Hard to imagine she had a cramp anywhere.

"Face-down for a start," Paul said. A little awkwardly, he affixed the cushioned donut to the front of the table. "If you could just... drop your head in there."

"Oh," said Lina, half-surprise, half-sigh. Many of his clients reacted so. Just the configuration of the table with the face ring was enough to take some pressure off upper back and neck problems. So Lina did have some trouble like that. Maybe she did.

Paul started easily, feathering out and up from the base of her spine. She sighed with the movement. "Do you want the robe off?"

"It's all right," he said, though ordinarily he'd go straight to the skin. But in this case, even with the thin weave of cotton between her and his fingertips, somehow her warmth elicited an unprofessional reaction. With her face in the donut, she couldn't know. Paul thought she couldn't, anyway. His position put Fuselli's "Nightmare" at his back, and straight ahead were those aristocratic women, Gabrielle d'Estrées and her sister, their skins so round and white and smooth there was almost nothing to delineate them. The sister had, with a pinch suggesting the universal okay sign, had captured the pink cylinder of Gabrielle's nipple between thumb and forefinger, manipulating it as she might the stem of a pomegranate, while Gabrielle herself, no sign in her small dark eyes of the least involvement with this touch, held out with a similar gesture a delicate ring with a dark jewel.

"Oh," said Lina, to the floor. "*Oh my.*"

"That's right, "Paul said. He'd made his way to her shoulders and there found a good knotty spasm after all, in the usual spot where the trapezius and the deltoid pulled on sternomastoid and the scaline (to mention just a few). There was decent amount of bursitis there too, crunching under his probing thumbs as he pushed through it, beginning to release the spasm into rolling, and "Oh," Lina said, more urgently, while Paul's voice struck a deeper note; "Good Girl," he said. "Good Girl,"—conscious all the while that his ankles were passing in front of the Plexiglass where the snakes were (he would have liked to handle the big yellow boa), aware also that although real Lina could not see him at all (well, maybe at this point the tips of his slippers) because her face was sinking deeper and deeper into the donut as he worked the arch of her neck, he was being regarded by many images of Lina festooned around the room, half-hidden by those scarves or artful coils of vine spun out of her planters, some indifferent, others shrewd, some about to burst forth with song or laughter.

"*O My God,*" Lina's phrase dissolved to moan, and Paul was working her neck's arch hard in the donut, chanting his usual patter, *see how it's rolling that must have really been hurting you, Good Girl, Good Girl, it's coming out now. Now then. There there.*

He took his hands away. Lina remained prone, for a moment, her face in the donut. A goldfinch swung in a tiny perch not far above the back of her head. Paul wondered how the whole place wasn't covered in guano. Marvelous clear light poured over the window seat (and it seemed to him it had been drizzling outside when he first entered the building). There were a number of oddly shaped and colored vials and cruets lining the windowsill, some with coils of herbs inside.

"Has it been an hour?" Lina said, rolling again to one side to face him. A peach-colored breast slipped from the slack join of her kimono; she didn't seem aware of it. Paul locked his eyes onto her green ones.

"High intensity," he said. "Goes fast. There's a couple of exercises I could—"

But Lina had swung her bare feet to the floor; with the movement the loose breast slipped back under the fabric. She smiled and glanced up at the bird swinging on the perch. "I had a kestrel in here for a while," she said. "You know, a little sparrow hawk?"

Paul nodded.

"But he ate all my little birds," Lina said. "Blood all over." She bit her lower lip and released it, visibly reddened. "Just a little blood, but still."

"What happened to the kestrel?" Paul said.

Lina moved toward him on the table, so that the *V* of her kimono nearly brushed his striped T-shirt. She made a gesture for raising the window sash and smiled. "He flew away," she said, with a laugh like chimes.

The yellow boa rolled around his forearm. It made itself smaller so it would fit, scaly tail tip licking into the slack skin inside his elbow, the blunt head arched away and turning back to explore his closed fist with a quick, no-touch dart of tongue. Its color lay somewhere between lemon and egg yolk, blushing toward yolk as it tightened and squeezed. The hot weight of snake made it hard for him to hold his arm upright, but the veins of his inner forearm were responding, pumping up to the surface to throb into the belly of the snake.

The boa had warmed to the heat of his skin. Now it contracted, coil by coil, a hot rhythm milking upward toward his wrist, repeating, until helplessly his fist bloomed open, releasing a blood-colored droplet, winged and flying. Another kind of bird.

Lina Liège did not call for a follow-up appointment. Paul was not necessarily surprised. He charged considerably more than the average masseur, on the assurance that fewer visits would be needed. Frequently a single treatment would suffice, combined with exercises he prescribed to stop a problem from recurring. In Lina's case he had done so, as usual, though he might, if he had thought of it, played out the therapeutic relationship a bit longer. One or two more visits would not have been out of line. Yet Paul had always been wary of the misread touch, transference, therapy slipping into seduction—he'd heard of people losing their licenses that way. The fact that he himself had never had a license didn't make him feel especially more secure.

So he had expected to forget the startling Ms. Liège, if a week or so went by and she didn't call.

On the way out he'd abstracted a card from a gold-rimmed bowl by the door. It looked as if he were meant to take it, where the bowl was placed, and yet for some reason he'd magicked it into his sleeve, like a pick-pocket. A Z from a magnetic poetry set pinned the card to his Brooklyn refrigerator, unless he took it down to look at it again. One side was a color photo of Lina in a sort of faintly period costume, posed on a small love seat, one high-heeled shoe cocked up on the arm rest and the other on the floor. There was a red drapery for background; the shot had not been taken in her apartment, he didn't think. The red brought up the pallor of her skin and thrust it forward.

On the flip, her name in Spencerian script, website, email, and phone number.

He kept thinking about the yellow boa, and how he would

like to have handled it. How long it had been since he picked up a snake.

At dusk he poured a short glass of rum and dialed her number from his kitchen, surprised when she answered so quickly, unprepared indeed.

How's that soldier, he said, in an utterly unconvincing attempt at an avuncular tone. *I mean shoulder.*

Oh, she said. *So it must be Paul.*

You remember me, he said, inanely. Her voice was lower than he remembered, with a sort of sweet viscosity to it; it seemed to wrap around his whole identity when she pronounced his name. He was pacing in his kitchen, looking out at the diner across the street. Twenty years before when he'd first moved in, the whole area was a dispiriting ghetto and the diner was vacant and gated by dark. Now it was a gourmet joint that drew half its customers out of Manhattan; the garden terrace was beginning to fill.

And you're calling about my shoulder. Lina seemed to be suppressing amusement of some kind. *My shoulder is good.*

Not really, Paul said. Although, now she mentioned it, he had a clear picture of her shoulder and how it had looked at the moment she'd rolled the towel he'd handed her around herself and tucked it up just under her armpits, leaving both her icewhite shoulders bare.

He took a sip of rum. *I'd like to see you,* he said. *Socially, I mean.*

In the following silence, he could hear the hum of the phone line. Then her musical laughter came.

You're just going to laugh at me, Paul said, without resentment. My God I think I'm in love, he was thinking. Or whatever it is that makes you lose your senses. *I mean, I would if I were you.*

Not at all. For the first time he thought he heard a trace of accent in her voice. *I'll see you.* She paused. On the diner's terrace they were lighting the lamps, whose yellowish glow fractured on his window pane.

Socially, Lina added, and he thought he could feel her smile.

Silence.

You seem to have my number, Lina said, and she hung up.

"Lina" is an excerpt from *Tombs,* a novel in progress.

A Love Affair

STEPHEN MCCAULEY

SHE KNEW that if it weren't for the strange and lovely summerhouse he and his wife owned, she would not be having an affair with him. Her passion for the house was genuine and unqualified, while her feelings for him were ambivalent. She could easily do without their afternoon encounters two or three times a month, but she couldn't bear the thought of no longer entering the rooms in which they had sex. Sometimes, the rooms appeared in her dreams; he never did. She worried that this meant she lacked warmth and empathy, but perhaps it was preferable to have fallen head over heels for a piece of real estate—a house the owners rarely used—rather than for another woman's husband.

When he told her one afternoon as they lay on the flowered sheets of the bed in the guestroom that he and his wife intended to put the house on the market, she felt a clutch of panic, almost as if someone were putting a hand over her nose and mouth and cutting off her oxygen.

"Why?" she asked in a voice that sounded stricken, even to her.

He misinterpreted her tone, and put his arms around her. "Don't worry," he said. "We'll figure out another place to meet. Maybe at your apartment when your roommate is at work?"

She'd just turned thirty and lived alone in a town about ten minutes from the house. She'd told him she had a roommate because the thought of being touched by him outside of these walls made her shudder.

"Maybe," she said.

The house had been built by an artist in the 1920's. It had never been properly winterized. Most of the systems were outdated and impractical. He'd claimed throughout the ten months they'd been seeing each other that he and his wife were planning to do major renovations, but they'd never gotten around to it. She had a feeling there were many things they never got around to. "Why hurry?" she had always encouraged when he spoke of making changes in the house.

There was something shabby about the décor—the faded chintz and brittle wicker inherited from the original owners—and rundown about the exterior; the shingles were weathered and crooked and the windows rattled and needed to be reglazed. The house was perched above a granite quarry now filled with clear, cold water that reflected and magnified the house's flaws. She couldn't explain her attraction—her obsession, really—any more than a friend at work could explain her love for a homely, dull man she'd alternately swooned and wept over for two years. She only knew that she was happy anticipating each visit and that each time she entered she felt she'd come home.

Once she'd managed to compose herself after his announcement about the sale and had started to get back into her clothes, she said, as casually as possible, "When?"

"Soon. Probably it will take a long time to find a buyer."

"Possibly," she said.

There was no question about her being able to afford it, even without knowing the price. She worked in development at a small museum in Salem. She loved the work she did, but her salary was minimal. She was going to have to learn to live without the house. She pulled up her jeans and gazed out the window at the surface of the water in the quarry. A breeze blew in from the ocean and formed widening ripples.

It was mid-September, but fall was already in the air.

· · · · · · ·

It wasn't a surprise that the house sold quickly. She didn't ask how many people had bid on it. Many, she preferred to think, feeling proud on behalf of the house itself.

When he told her the closing date, she decided to get it over with immediately. She did not believe in prolonging the inevitable.

"I didn't mention this before," she said, "but I got offered a job at a small museum in San Francisco. I'm moving in two weeks. I'm afraid I won't be able to see you again."

It wasn't something he could argue with, and maybe in the long run, it was a relief to him, too. He wasn't a bad person.

· · · · · · ·

They'd always met on Wednesday afternoons because it was easy for her to get out early that day. After she stopped seeing him, she felt herself growing anxious and melancholy as the middle of the week approached. She'd sit in her office thinking about the four o'clock shadows crossing the cracked linoleum of the kitchen, about the oversized fireplace that needed repointing, and about what the light might look like at this moment, coming through the dimpled glass of the guestroom window. To calm herself, she began to drive to the house and sit on the porch, gazing out at the quarry with her back pressed against the bleached shingles. The visits soothed her and made her happy, although she knew they'd have to end soon.

One afternoon, as she was walking from the porch to her car, an SUV pulled into the drive, followed by a pickup truck. A man got out of the former and looked at her quizzically, as if she were a trespasser, and needed to explain her presence.

"I was just ... walking around the quarry," she stammered.

He seemed to accept that. "My wife and I closed on the

house yesterday," he said. He pointed to the truck. "My contractor is here to look at a few things we're going to have done."

"Of course. Major renovations?"

"Oh, no," he said. "I love it as is."

In her nervousness at having been caught, she hadn't paid much attention to his appearance. Now, she saw that he was probably about the same age as her former lover, and while not handsome, appealing in a relaxed, middle-aged way. There were things about him she could imagine one day finding attractive.

She put out her hand and introduced herself. "I've always wondered what inside of this house looked like," she said. "Would you mind if I came in with you?"

I Love Nothing Like the Tuba

ELIZABETH GRAVER

First Year Writing Seminar: What's Your Passion?

I LOVE NOTHING LIKE THE TUBA. I play it in Marching Band. My tuba is shiny, silver, huge/gigantic/colossal/great[1]. Look at you go, boy, says my dad after. During, he sits in the luxury box with the other Donors. I don't mean heart, I don't mean kidney, but he'd do it for me if I needed one, he'd give me his left foot and get around, ha ha, on a bloody stump. Secret: I don't play it. The ones who play get a full college ride but there's not enough of them and they cost too much so the school brings us in because tubas are peppy, pepalicious, *visually exiting*. Secret, spell check sucks, spellcheck suks, don't depend on it! You are in COLLAGE. Remember to print and read aloud PEN IN HAND!!!! You get 500 pages a year for "free." Secret, my tuba isn't real, not fake either, it EXISTS (me too) but is fiberbrass, aka fiber with a brass silver-plated bell. It weighs 25 pounds which is alot a lot allot. Mucho. Bow-coo. I get tired, I am often very tired. The real tuba players call me Tupperware Toilet Bowl Plastic Bugle, despite brass/silver-plate. Also Flaming Tuba. Haha, score me some propane. Secret: it's a sousaphone, not a tuba. Look it up. In high school I had 10 passions (see Common App): Model UN, 3D modeling, model ships/males models/model trains, etc. Model: mod· el, mädl/noun, *three-dimensional representation of a person or thing or of a pro-*

1 Thesaurus.com

posed structure, typically on a smaller scale than the original: "A model of St. Paul's Cathedral."[2] My dad says "Get out there and march, Junior, give it your all, I'm damn proud of you." It's where he went to, we're the Screaming Gophers, you can see us on TV during the games. Secret: not playing the tuba is a s*** ton of work. Get up for practice, lug case, hold instrument up to sky. There's parade rest, horns up, right face, left face, halt, left flank, backwards march. After the game I shine the bell with Hagerty Silversmiths Polish with Tarnish Prevention and put my good tuba to sleep on its flank in its plushy case. It gets tired. It is often very tired. *flank noun\ flanjk 1: the fleshy part of the side between the ribs and the hip. She gently patted the horse's flank. 2: a cut of meat from this part of an animal—see BEEF ILLUSTRATION.*[3] The football guys have tight rear ends, backsides, seats, buttocks, rumps, derrieres. The fans cheer and cheer, and sometimes for me. All in all, I love nothing like the tuba.

2   https://en.oxforddictionaries.com/definition/model
3   https://www.merriam-webster.com/dictionary/flank

The Brunt

JOHN LILLY

We're older by a year each time the photographs emerge.
The Art Cars ply the Playa, yet another demiurge
commands the wheel in goggles, writhing diodes, penis sock,
for he is older too but young at heart about Black Rock.

But old—as old as one becomes, confronted year-by-year
with all the antic majesty. And who will shed a tear?
The desiccated mermaids won't, nor will they sing to me
should I at last attend a decade late or two or three,
my trousers rolled in deference to insinuating dust,
no longer young enough at heart to revel in the lust,

the drugs.... I'll give away the peaches I don't care to eat
and bark a raspy "welcome home," as one is to repeat,
and in the gritty wind they'll take my grimace for a grin
and take a dusty bite, and I'll be outside looking in....
Who won't be wanting out by then, some days into the week?
Between the noise and narcissists, the too-insistent freaks,
and everywhere the beauty of the desert's ruthless pan
and me who won't have seen it when at last they burn the Man.

The Snipe Hunt

JOHN LILLY

Or there's the royal-wedding walkabout
my in-law sent me on in '95
to find her son, who hadn't yet appeared.
(I try to keep this stuff relatable.)
Seville Cathedral, ninety in the shade:
a morning-coated fool-errant strides
cell-phoneless past the barricaded throng,
the sweat collecting, drenching, seeping through
my cutaway as I complete the turn,
the circuit, having craned my way around
and come up short. A frenzied widow waves
and in my fog I half-approach. She shouts
in Andalusian Spanish, "Who are *you*?"
"I'm no one. An unknown American."
Let down, she says I'm handsome—touchingly.
Relatability is in the tale,
its elements. Whose in-laws *haven't* sent
them out for ice or coffee, out for beer
or out to find someone who wasn't there?

Sunflower State

JOHN LILLY

All we are, they sang to us, is dust:
everything is dust in the wind. I know
it's true; we didn't know but thought we did.

Recall sixth grade, that town, the tiled walls.
I do. I summon seventy-seven's smells—
the Charlie-scented halls, Bazooka-chewed—
and sounds, the Kansan sounds of Illinois.
And into summer: soccer, summer camp
and root beer on a Boundary Waters lake.
Duluth packs in a rod-long Grumman. Loons.
Then Montreal and toffee, Mackintosh.
Quebec. The Plains of Abraham. *Arrêt.*

With Elvis dead, that fall would be my last
full fall. That fall would be the last for us:
the next we'd go and start the scattering.
New job, a move. The girl to Iowa,
to school. (Remember that? Remember now?)

The name of this band wasn't Talking Heads.
Carry on, they seemed to sing, my wayward son:
you're only done when dust and peace are one.

Wrong Yoga

KARAN MAHAJAN

OF ALL THE TYPES OF YOGA PRACTICED IN THE US TODAY—
Hatha yoga, Ashtanga vinyasa yoga, Bikram yoga—the one that
I enjoy most happens to be the one that I invented. I like to call
this type of yoga "wrong yoga."

Wrong yoga began one morning on a mat in my apartment
on Clinton Avenue, in a burning square of light supplied by my
east-facing window. My practice soon moved down to the lawn
in front of my building, where I felt I could show off all the
wrong moves I had developed to the men and women pouring
into the neighborhood for the Saturday flea market.

There are many ways of communicating in New York. One
is through the names of Wi-Fi networks. On my block, these
included YO!APT202TurnOFFtheKENNY_G, NghbrhdYOGA-
CLOWN, 2PAC&UPaki, and NOCARBS4ME, all of which must
have cut high-frequency arcs through my body as I did yoga.
Another way of communicating is through the middle finger,
which New Yorkers eagerly brandish at any car trying to do
basic car things like make a yellow light. And the third and
perhaps most ubiquitous form of communication in the city is
conversation about yoga.

You will be surprised by how many lonely women—and
men—will stop to talk to you if you do wrong yoga in your
building's front yard (the rarity of the front yard itself never
to be remarked on). Even the usual laws of yoga conversation
don't explain it. Is it possible that certain women have an urge
to correct a wayward yogi the way they have an urge to correct those of us who have unruly personalities? Or is it some-

thing simpler: the sight of an individual debasing himself so thoroughly in public attracting curiosity the way an accident attracts gawkers?

As the spring gave way to summer, I began to see that I had acquired a sort of superpower. The more I hurt myself with these obscene postures, the more attention I attracted. Excited by this development, I began to go down to the Za'atar House Middle Eastern restaurant and discuss the matter with the head waiter, Mina.

Mina, who was in his late thirties, was an Egyptian, but he had an indeterminate Aryan look about him. He was the leading expert on lonely women in the neighborhood. Whenever I came to the restaurant, he served me a vegetable kebab platter and another objectionable story about his conquests. He always left my table to go kiss another one of his svelte customers on the cheek. Mina, I found out later, was a Coptic Christian; he'd emigrated to the US from Egypt because he wanted to coach soccer in schools. Things turned out differently. When he arrived in Queens, he found that being gifted at soccer wasn't enough to become a coach. You also needed English. He struggled with the language, went at it, punched holes in it, tried to breathe against the gush of his Arabic instincts—I imagined him down in the water in a sack, struggling like Houdini—but it was no use. English evaded him. He could strut around like a cock in his restaurant and flirt with women, but he was basically crippled. In the meantime, he searched for work in the Arabic-language schools in Brooklyn. And here, too, like a cruel joke, the same prejudices he must have fled in Egypt asserted themselves. "The Muslim guys don't want a Christian to coach," he said in a matter-of-fact way.

Strangely, I didn't feel bad for him. He was too shifty, too unreliable in his attentions, and when he spoke to me it was always with one eye on a woman in the corner. "He's happy," I thought. "He's mourning soccer because it makes him a tragic figure, but he's really quite happy." On my block there was even a Wi-Fi network worshipfully named after him.

Then, one day, long after the Arab Spring had ended, I asked him how things were back home, whether he planned to return. "Maybe, Brother," he said. But his look was vacant, even accusatory, the look of someone who has been caught out. And it occurred to me that, though the Spring was a source of pride in Egypt, it had only reminded this man, stuck in the purgatory of his restaurant, that he was missing out on things back home (though, being a Copt, even that was complicated). And perhaps this has been the source of his exasperation all along—not soccer, not English, not women, but something personal and sad keeping him from Egypt all these years. I disliked myself for not having noticed it before.

Soon after this conversation I fell into a depression. I had seen it coming all spring and summer, had seen it rippling on the whorls in my old windows, had felt it in my tense postures on the grass, and then, just like that, I was in it. I gave up yoga and went back to my room with its crazily sloping floors. I sat before the window in my office chair and thought back to childhood, which is where the mind travels when it is afraid of death.

I had been obsessed with cricket as a young man in India. I loved the game but I also cherished the statistics, the equipment, the boredom, the tea. Yet, as I sat at the window, it was not the sport with its pleasant longueurs that came back to me, but rather something else, something more specific, the image of a single boy: Sharad. Sharad, one of the richest people I have ever met, was an awful fellow. Having inserted himself into my ragtag group of teenage cricketers in the neighborhood park, he proceeded to disperse his servants, six of them, among our teams like spies. These servants were nice enough fellows, only a little older than us, but they were terrified of Sharad, and if you got one on your team you could guarantee that he was playing not for you but for his little master.

We put up with Sharad because he supplied us with the equipment—pads and bats and bails—and also because his parents were divorced, and we felt pity for him. But Sharad tested our pity. He cheated and argued about scores. He bowled purposely at our faces and insulted his servants. He ridiculed the weaker players. And then, one day, after a terrible row about a run out (he felt, naturally, that he was not out), he strode out of the park, marched into a side street, and complained to a neighborhood official about our cricketing in the park.

A white-haired man with sucked-in cheeks appeared at the rusted green fence of the park. "Beta, the rules on the plaque say that no cricket or sporting activities are permitted here," he said. Where had he been all this time? It was technically a "walking" and "strolling" park, one of those places where middle-aged paunchy people fool themselves into thinking that a thirty-minute daily amble will cancel out a lifetime of sedentary sweetmeat-eating.

We thought the man, one of the neighborhood "uncles," would disappear into his own laziness, but Sharad must have persisted. We were pushed out. Within days, the bald expanse in the middle of the park, where we dug our wickets, was peppered over with young green grass. Wooden benches with iron legs clogged the grounds. Petunias and phlox began to arrogantly bloom in the empty beds around the walking paths; the paths themselves filled with the sluggish diabetics of our parents' generation.

All Sharad's doing! Over a run out!

All these years, I had never forgiven him, but now, sitting in my bed in Brooklyn, I wanted nothing more than to switch places with Sharad, to be cruel like Sharad, to be a person who injured others instead of injuring himself. Outside, fall was ending.

The fall had started with fevers, with people coughing into their sleeves on the subway, with fairs, with couples fighting on the street. Now winter brought its bitterness and cold and toxic metal scents, and I felt again the strange need I always felt—especially when I was depressed—to move. I packed up my things. I ate one last time at the Za'atar House, where Mina refused to talk to me. The patch of lawn where I'd performed wrong yoga was blank with snow.

The new apartment was in Park Slope and had elegant pressed-tin ceilings with floral designs: carnations, I think. When I moved in, the landlady pointed out a niche in the first-floor landing. "When people died in these houses," she said cheerfully, "the wakes used to be held in the living room. You needed the niche, or you couldn't get the coffin up these narrow stairs." She directed me to put my stuff in the attic, which was so low I had to crawl. "People used to live there, you know," she said. I believed it.

Soon after, having stowed away my things, I got my espresso maker going on the stove. After two weeks, I began to feel settled. I brought out my mat. It was then that I discovered that the pressed-tin ceilings of the apartment were too low; too low for right yoga and too low for wrong yoga, and I experienced a deep panic. My ex-girlfriends had always said that I made decisions too fast and there was a great deal of truth to that. I'd never lived in an apartment I liked, never thought to examine such things as the water pressure in the shower or the heat in the bedroom when I moved in. When I decided, I just decided.

I was grateful that I was alone so that no one knew that I had screwed up. This is the main benefit of being alone.

But the panic! The panic I experienced that night in the absence of my wrong yoga was frightening. And it was then, breathing through my mouth, that I decided to go out for a walk in the middle of the night.

It was moonlit outside, snowing, the city's million conversations blotted out by the rhythmic exhalation of the falling snow. I put one foot before the other on the pavement. I felt the panic inside me balanced by the cold outside. And I waited, as I took my first steps in this new setting, for something bad to happen, for my foot to slip or my ankle to twist, for something to free me for a moment from myself and make me what I had been when I had come into this world, a happy howling animal.

"Wrong Yoga" originally appeared in *VQR*.

The Next Right Thing

ELIZABETH WURTZEL

I STARTED PROZAC NATION IN 1986, after my freshman year of college. It was supposed to be an article about Harvard's 350th anniversary for *New York* magazine. It was something like 20,000 words, so it didn't work as an article. Of course *The New Yorker* has famously run 20,000 words on wheat—but how can I compete with wheat? It was about my experiences at Harvard. A lot of that is in the book, but I don't know if anything from the original piece is in there exactly.

I described large amounts of drug use and promiscuity—and for some reason people find that shocking. People *still* find that shocking. When you say that kids are using a lot of drugs and are promiscuous in college, people are like, *so what?* But when you tell the whole crazy story, the acid-trip details of it all, people are always shocked. People are shocked by young people behaving like young people. I don't know why, but there's an endless, bottomless audience for material about young people who are probably going to end up just fine, but are right now behaving like idiots, because it's what young people do. I don't know if it's still what young people do, because the world is more conservative.

I just don't think there are large amounts of cocaine on campuses now the way there was in 1985.

And I don't know that there were ever large quantities of cocaine at Harvard.

But I encountered large quantities of cocaine.
I don't think everyone did. I believe most people did not.
But I did.
It was just what we did when we had parties. It went on
every weekend. And sometimes on weekdays.
Okay, so it went on all the time wherever I went. If you
asked me, Harvard was a coke den.
I guess I thought I could give wheat a run for its money.
Writing has been good for me because whenever I needed to
find something to do, because I ran out of things to do, I would
find the thing to do. I just always did the next right thing.
I was working at the *Dallas Morning News* in the summer of
1988. It was the second summer I was there. I was working in
the style section, writing features about stars and bars. I wrote
an article in which I made up all the quotes. It was never published. Before it ran, I told them about it. It was a dating article,
and no one was giving me good quotes—it's often the problem
that no one has anything good say, not just in journalism, but
all the time. I turned myself in before it ran. Which was a good
thing, compared to how much worse it could have been. But
there I was in Dallas sometime in August, and I did not have
a job anymore. There was a literary agent in Dallas who somehow had huge clients, because there are so many good people
writing in Texas. There are so many *people* in Texas. Somebody
I knew knew her, so I gave her this old thing I had. And she
thought, *Yes, it could be a book.*
I know that sounds all too easy. But I have a feeling that is
mostly how these things happen. Talent is not an unobvious
thing. Talent screams out. Talent excites people. Anyone having trouble getting noticed is probably not talented, and should
likely not be trying.
I spent a lot of my senior year in college in meetings with
publishers who wanted to buy the book. The idea was it was
going to be a book about Harvard.

It was sold to Crown as a book about Harvard. I can't remember why that didn't work out, but then Morgan Entrekin at Grove Atlantic bought it from Crown. Or maybe Crown never bought it. So much happened that I can't remember exactly what happened.

Morgan had long floppy hair and tortoiseshell glasses. He was surely the worst person for me to work with. Morgan was having an affair with Diandra Douglas, Michael Douglas' wife. He was an unrepentant womanizer, but because everyone wants what they can't have, Morgan was in an obsessive way with Diandra. He would get upset about whatever was going on with her, and he would take to his bed. I would call him at home during the day, and this was back when there was call waiting and answering machines, and the telephone would ring and ring, but he would not pick up, because he was on the phone with Diandra. This was during the workday.

It was impossible to work with someone like that.

Morgan was good friends with Jay McInerney and Gary Fisketjon, Jay's editor, and they were on a massive coke binge. For a long time. Morgan could have been a serious person in some way—he probably is a serious person. But he was just utterly unstable, in the way you would be if you did cocaine all the time. I knew something about that, having lived through 1985, but by 1989 I could not believe it. Morgan was exasperating. If a woman behaved like him, she would be living under scaffolding and begging for change in a world that is done with cash. Same with all of them. Men, that is.

In the meantime, I wrote an article for *Mademoiselle*, about my experiences with Prozac, and I had the idea that would be a better book. It wouldn't be so different. Actually, it would be exactly the same. I could not work with Morgan, and my agent resold the book to Simon & Schuster. By now I was catching on. The idea was to say anything. It was a *yeah yeah yeah* world. I was 22 and I already knew it. This time my agent sold it as a book about recovering from a bad depression on Prozac. By that time it had become the book it is now. But it was always the same thing. I only ever write one thing: I write about what I see.

I see interesting things.

The negotiations along the way are a hassle. The book would be done and in stores and bringing in money in all the time I have spent on conversations about it that are mostly because—because what? I did not convince you when you knew?

When people think these things go easily, they don't know. They don't. It has never been easy to be a writer not named Jonathan or David or James.

By this time, I was out of college. First I was the pop music critic at *New York* magazine, then I was the pop music critic at *The New Yorker*. I got my job at *The New Yorker* by calling the editor and saying I wanted a job. And from talking to me, he could tell I meant business. Anybody can send anybody an email, but there are things you can convey in a phone call that are lost online. Nowadays in offices the phone doesn't ring anymore. No one ever calls anyone. It would probably work to call whoever you want now, because no one calls at all. We've moved into a world of avoiding confrontation, and as a result confrontation is really effective.

Try it.

I gave the manuscript to Bob Gottlieb, who was the editor of *The New Yorker* at the time. I felt like there was a problem with Simon & Schuster, that they had not been adequately supportive. There was a space of time between *New York* magazine and *The New Yorker*, so I wasn't working and I ran out of money. It was typical back then that if a publisher believed in the project, they would give you a piece of the rest of your advance, if you needed money to live on. And I couldn't get Simon & Schuster to do that. Bob Gottlieb had been editor in chief at Knopf for many years, so he was in a good position to judge, and he told me that was terrible of them, that I should leave there, that it wasn't a good relationship. Who knows? As it happens, Bob is great. He's utterly great. So I thought it was probably good advice, especially because he was on my side. I'm always happy to walk away from someone who's not nice to me. I had an editor at Simon & Schuster who was very old fashioned. Someone else would have got me the money. But her feeling was: Go waitress. Maybe she was right. But that was not what I wanted to hear. I was young, and why not another publisher? I was getting used to the idea that this was going to be completely ridiculous.

Then the president of *The New Yorker*, a man named Steve Florio, sent me to Mort Janklow, the legendary literary agent. It was a Monday in August and I called him. He was supposed to be in South Hampton, but he wasn't, so he had a blank day. So I met him. Mort's office is in Midtown on Park Avenue, and has a lot of black lacquer. It is very Hollywood. He is charming as all get out. We got along famously, and he took me on. And this started all over again.

Finally the book was sold to Houghton Mifflin for $50,000. It was not a big deal to get me out of the Simon & Schuster contract. Mort resold the book. He sent it to a bunch of editors and it was the same thing all over again. By then it was more serious. I had written for *The New Yorker* so it was all more serious. Not like it wasn't before. I talked to a lot of people, entertained all these offers, had a good idea about publishing before I was done with college, and the thing you need to know is that I am a flawed person in all these ways but I know how to write, so that did not surprise me.

Even still, it was difficult.

Nobody could understand why I wanted to do a memoir. Various times it came up that the book that became *Prozac Nation* ought to be a sociological study. I just thought it was a memoir. It seemed like that's what it should be. I definitely thought I could include some statistics. But it just didn't seem interesting to do something else. It didn't seem like I should turn it into a novel, because it was all true. But no one thought the idea of a memoir was very good. The title, *Prozac Nation*, is deliberately deceptive: It sounds like it is anything but a memoir. No one could imagine that anyone would be interested in the life of a twentynothing.

There weren't reality stars at the time. There wasn't a population of people just famous for being themselves. All that stuff was yet to happen. You couldn't invent yourself on Instagram. There wasn't so much imaginary life. You were doing something or you weren't. You couldn't just tweet about nothing. Everything else was suggested besides a memoir. *Everything* else. But Betsy Lerner, who was an editor at the time at Houghton Mifflin, just got it. She understood, and was completely into it.

My orientation was pop music. I learned how to write from listening to songs. I learned how to be a writer from rock 'n roll. It was all about cult of personality. If I loved an artist, I bought all his albums, because I was invested in the ongoing story. Confessional poetry had once sold well—Sylvia Plath and Anne Sexton were celebrities—but that was replaced by Bob Dylan and Joni Mitchell offering the same experience in song. I figured the only way to win over an audience was by being that honest and bare. I wanted readers to be attached to me. I knew that was the way to do it. I knew a memoir was perfect.

I lived on 18th and Park, and Houghton Mifflin was across the street on 18th and Park. So I used to just show up at Betsy's office, like every day. I would just kind of wander in. There was no security and nobody stopped me. I would show up there in sweatpants having just rolled out of bed. I was in my early twenties. And somehow we did this.

But it took me a very long time before I could actually sit down and write the book, because I would end up in these devastating relationships. Chris Whitley was one of them. Chris was an amazing Texas guitar player, the kind they only make in the Great State of Texas, and he was signed to the same label as Bob Dylan and Billie Holiday. I first saw him play his National steel at the Bell Cafe in SoHo, and he was shockingly talented. He wasn't going to be a rock star: he *was* a rock star. He was born that way. It was an amazing thing to behold someone so gifted. It was hard to imagine what he did in his spare time. I could not figure out why he talked or walked—it seemed like he ought to just fly around. He was that super-duper. Have you ever seen a bald eagle fly with nine feet of wingspan? It's something that shouldn't exist in nature, and it barely exists on a Boeing, and yet: it flies. There it is in the sky. Wow! That is how good he was.

Anyway, to quote Steve Earle: *You know the rest.* I would never flatter myself by saying I was a groupie. No, I was nothing quite that awesome. I was just plain crazy. And I somehow learned to live with the way Chris drank Old Granddad Kentucky bourbon by the bottle-after-bottle and picked fights with the lamps in the living room. I don't know if he liked to toss them around because they were bright, because they were slender, because they reminded him of someone he used to love—or simply because they did not punch back. After a few months of boxing with all things illuminating, he blessedly moved on, and I cried night and day. But it turns out Betsy had been involved with him too. Can you imagine? She found him playing on the street. Ah, I had her. I now knew she was a mess. Mess is a thing that runs deep in people. It's the chronic. I could see the knots in her hair that would never be soft. Yes she understood me, but more to the point, I got her. Betsy would figure out what I meant with my color-coded Post-its, my underlines and notes in a ROYGBIV-array of inks.

But I had to actually get the book written. Somehow.

Finally what happened is I have this friend Peter, and I went to his parents' house in Boca Raton—it was in Boca Village or Boca West, one of these huge developments. I stayed with them. I would write for a few hours every morning, and then I would go to Town Center, which was the mall with a Saks and A Nathan's Hot Dogs. I would look forward all morning to a frankfurter with onions. There were a few places in Boca Raton I liked going, so I would do that in the afternoon. And by doing this, by writing for a few hours every day and going to the mall, in a few weeks I got an awful lot of it done.

There it is, the whole trick of it: not Yaddo, but a condominium complex in Boca that is walking distance to the mall.

Okay so ... the trick is to stay away from anything like a writers' colony or a place where you are going to have to be with people and their issues. Like you ever need that. But as irresistible as that mostly is all the wretched time, only a really nice shopping mall will do when you are writing a book, because it's the worst.

Writing is the bad part of writing and there are no good parts.

So then I came home and I kept working. Once you get started on something it's not hard to keep it going. It's hard to get started. That is the whole trick. As a writer, I work with my hands, because the most meaningful gesture is typing at all.

But looking back the thing that amazes me is that I didn't really want to write a book. I just lost my job at the *Dallas Morning News*, and I needed something to do. It all started because I'd written this thing for *New York* magazine, and it was sitting there. And I parlayed that into the next thing. I just looked around and thought what have I got to offer? Everybody always likes stories about Harvard. I have plenty of those. I'll sell out my friends, I don't care. Publishing is pretty stupid. It's stupider than most stupid things. I was not hoping to get my life aligned with it. I wanted to be a rock star, but that's not what I'm good at. See, I'm not crazy. I don't drive myself crazy trying to do things I'm not good at. I'm just sensible.

When I was in high school, I loved *New York* magazine. And

I thought it would be great to write for *New York* someday. That had to have been the best job ever. And I just thought maybe someday I could do that. I didn't want to write a book. I didn't have any big plans. *The New Yorker* was not in my plans. I just needed to make money, and when I ran out of money I had to find new ways to make money. And it turned out my best bet was writing a book.

Heaven knows I never wanted to write a novel. I read *Lolita*, and I thought: English is not Nabokov's first language and he came up with this. So now why is anyone still trying to write novels? The greatest novel possible has been done. There wasn't much more you could do with a novel after *Lolita*. I didn't have great literary aspirations, that wasn't it. I thought I was good with words, I was good at writing, and that's how I wanted to live my life. I just wanted to be able to pay the rent as a writer.

I'd been told all my life that you couldn't make a living as a writer. I would tell people, I want to be a writer, and they would say, But what will you do instead? Because that's not going to work. No one was encouraging about this. I had terrible people in my life who did not encourage me. My family, them, those people—they were really bad about that. Whatever I wanted to do, people told me I couldn't do it. When I said I wanted to go to Harvard, they would tell me how hard it is to get into Harvard. And I would think to myself, *Yeah I know.*

This is stunning to me. I am a willful person, obviously, and people told me all the time about the things I could not do. And I am one of those people who can do anything, and that should have been obvious. I wanted to say, *I do difficult. I am in the business of difficult.*

But because I thought it would be a rare and exalted thing to make a living as a writer, that was all I ever wanted. I got an internship at *New York* when I was in high school, because I was really scared it wouldn't work out. I was really scared it was this impossible thing. I thought it was the hardest thing ever. I can't believe people go into this now, and want to be writers or whatever, and don't have a sense of awe about it. I thought to simply be able to get paid to write was a fucking miracle. So that's what I was hoping for. I would even write for a trade magazine about sewing. I thought I wanted to write for a newspaper. I could only think of writing in terms of a job. I just wanted my job to be writing.

And I have to say: I am so smart. Because that is really smart. That's what people should think. About whatever it is. Because it turns out that you can do anything you want with that. If your whole thing is, I need to pay the rent and I want to do it this way because this is what I'm good at, so much will develop from that. Or it did in my case.

I believe I was underestimating myself. Clearly I was underestimating myself. But I'd been brought up to underestimate myself—or to underestimate the world. The world had more opportunities than I realized. I see this now with people who go to Yale Law School and think the only job they can get is at a firm. They don't realize they can do anything, including something having nothing to do with law. It's an incredible credential, and they have such a small idea of what their lives can be. But it turns out having had a rather small idea of it, I had to keep figuring out ways to work it out. And I worked hard, and I was serious about it.

But if your whole goal is to make sure you pay your rent—and I was not limiting this to just food on the table—I think I cooked for the first time last week. Although at that time I was eating at MacDonald's plenty. I wasn't that fussy. But if that's what you're thinking, you might get quite far with it. Because life will constantly throw you curveballs, and you have to keep thinking of ways to make it all work. It seems unbelievable that the way I had to work it out was to write a book.

But I'd been at *The New Yorker*, and Tina Brown took over

and didn't want me to stay, so what else could I do? It seems like that was what I was meant to do, because I couldn't hold down a job.

Quite a lot happened, but I didn't plan it that way. All these people want to write great books, and they're crazy. That's no way to think of it. If you think I have to do this because I have to do something, you're good. I was not thinking it at the time, I did not feel driven by money, I was thinking I want to be a writer. But I realize now that the economy of writing has fallen apart so much, that being driven by the need to make a living is what should drive everybody all the time no matter what it is. Because if you're good, that's the answer. You should not be driven by immortality. You should not be driven by a need to write great works. You should not even be driven by a need to write at all—that's the one thing you don't want to be driven by. Because who needs to write?

If you're driven by, I need to find something to do because I need to fill my days and I need to pay my rent, you'll just keep coming up with ways of doing it because you have no other choice. Being driven by no other choice—people do their best work under those circumstances. You'll always try to be appealing. You'll always try to do a good job, because someone needs to pay you. You'll be thinking about the right things. You'll think about serving other people. You're never doing it just to make yourself happy. You're doing it because you think the world needs it. People should only write books that they can't imagine couldn't exist. You should not be writing because you feel like it. You have to think, *How is the world living without this?*

I had so many false starts. There were a million opportunities for me to give up. And that really is the trick—not being discouraged. But I couldn't be discouraged, because I needed something to do. I always ended up coming back to it, because it was my next best move.

If you don't know what to do, do the next right thing. And people often do the next wrong thing. People really ruin their lives by doing the next wrong thing.

But I was like, this didn't work, now what? But if I had a plan to write great literature, what a disaster. People have lost their minds and wasted their time trying to produce great literature. But if your whole thing is, I can't starve, you'd be stunned with what you come up with. You'll be thinking of what you need, not what you want.

You'll definitely come up with the next right thing.

"The Next Right Thing" originally aired (in different form) on the BBC.

Concord Free Press Interview

JORDY ROSENBERG

The Concord Free Press interviewed novelist Jordy Rosenberg in the Lenox Hotel after his appearance at the 2018 Boston Book Fair, where he read from *Confessions of the Fox*, his *astonishing and mesmerizing*[1] first novel. Instead of talking about writing his fantastic novel, being a transgender author-scholar, or teaching eighteenth-century literary and queer/transgender theory at the University of Massachusetts Amherst, we mostly talked about his childhood and family—which made him uncomfortable at first. He got over it.

Tell us a little about your family background—where are you from?

I grew up in New York City on 69th and 2nd Avenue in a rent-controlled apartment in one of those very anonymous postwar buildings. My father worked for the city in the Department of Public Health. My mother had many different jobs. She was mostly an administrative assistant. The last job she had was receptionist for a Park Avenue plastic surgeon for about ten to fifteen years. So she knew all the secrets of enhancement.

---

[1]   From the *Publishers Weekly* starred review, one of many enthusiastic reviews to *Confessions of the Fox*.

Was she herself enhanced?

Her boss was kind of a sleazeball. He would offer to test out new things on her. Meaning she was very happy to get it, you know. She was a real old-school yenta.

Were you the kind of kid who got around and explored the whole city?

It was amazing to grow up in New York City in the late Seventies and then Eighties. The Eighties were my teenager-dom. Yeah, I mean, we had total autonomy.

Where did you hang out?

I roamed down to areas I thought of as either punk or queer. Like 99X. I went to the music club CBGB a lot. I was listening to a lot of ska. Used to see Fishbone at CBGB. For some reason, I fell in with ska people. I don't know how it happened. I did a lot of roaming to queer things. I was kind of a loner. Not a loser, but I liked to spend a lot of time alone, so I would just walk around. There was the Oscar Wilde Bookshop in the West Village then, where I would just plant myself, looking for women—and there weren't many who went into that bookshop.

Do you remember your childhood as good, bad, or indifferent?

I felt very lucky to be growing up in New York City, because no matter how much you differed from your parents you could always just go out and walk on the street. I had a very strained relationship with my mother who, as a hardcore yenta, had very rigid gendered expectations for me. I went to the Spence School on a partial scholarship. So it was very intense. It was the Eighties, and all these girls were in my class—Jade Jagger,

Tatiana von Fürstenberg, and the Crown Princess of Greece. So it was very weird to be interacting with them, but I had gone to Spence since I was six, so it was supposed to be natural. I didn't really mind it because I always enjoyed the company of women. I think my mother wanted the etiquette lessons of Spence for me, but that didn't really work.

You seem very polite.

What I mean is, the feminine interpolation didn't work on me. It probably had the opposite effect. I was just around very intriguing girls all the time. It was totally thrilling, but maybe not in the way that it was supposed to be. My first novel was a private school girl tell-all novel that I then threw out and denounced. I made like a Marxist denunciation of it.

You *self-denounced* your first novel?

Yes. I was in my twenties I wrote it. And by then I had an agent. She was right about the direction it should have gone in. But I couldn't swallow it, and so I left it behind.

What was it called?

Oh, God.

Come on, Jordy.

It was called *That's Verboten, Kitten*. It's not necessarily a good title. I was in my twenties. It was kinda like speculative fiction, queer *Gossip Girl*, pseudo murder mystery.

We desperately want to read this book.

Oh, no.

Hope you saved it somewhere.

I think some exes might have hard copies, and I really hope that they don't surface. That book should never see the light of day. I didn't really fall in love with novels again until after I finished *Confessions of the Fox*. I wish that I'd been able to write it out of a feeling of being in love with fiction. But I had almost suspended that feeling while actually writing a novel.

There's a Czeslaw Milosz quote that goes: *When a writer is born into a family, the family is finished.* Did you always feel like you were a writer when you were growing up? And how did becoming a writer affect your family?

I guess I always wanted to be a writer. But I kind of put that aside. When I went to college, it was clear that my relations with my parents—particularly my mother—were deteriorating and I became very anxious about job security. I just couldn't deal with the anxiety that becoming a writer would have meant at that time, financially, I guess. So, at the time it seemed like becoming a professor was more stable. That was my plan. I was going to become a professor and get tenure—this was back when the tenure system was more intact. And *then* write. I was always writing on the side, but it wasn't my main thing. I fell in love with theory and philosophy.

But you had a plan.

Yes, and it didn't seem like a terrible plan to me. I think a lot of writers have games they play with themselves about what they can and can't have. I think at the time I thought I'd like to have a job, but I can't have fiction. Surviving and doing what you want to do—it's like a made-up trade that you make with the universe. And nobody cares.

One of the many things we really admire about your work is that even though you're a scholar who obviously admires theory and covers a lot of serious territory in his work—you're still okay making a joke now and then. You have a great sense of humor. Were you always funny?

I think so. Though she could be very difficult, my mother was also very, very funny in the way of yentas.

You did a great impersonation of your mother in one of your interviews.

I'm interested in that kind of dying language of Yiddish shtick, so I am really interested in forms of humor writing and forms of vernacular speech that communicate to a broader audience than standard academic fare. Or mixing the two. A lot of current academic writing—for good reasons, or depressing reasons—is about *brilliant theories of the worst-case scenario.* There's not really a place for Utopian theorizing anymore. And I think part of the drive for fiction is to preserve or extrapolate that Utopian drive that originally attracted me to academia.

The foundation shifted while you were standing on it.

I think that's true. I find impossible to express certain Utopian thoughts in scholarly writing now.

But fiction lets you do whatever you want. It's like dessert after the meat and potatoes.

Yeah, that's kind of my attitude right now.

Does it feel like freedom to you?

I don't know if I would describe it as *freedom*. I mean that's what I always say to students—we have to do all the hard stuff first and then I'll let you have fun. That's obviously just a projection of my own unconscious. And by the way, I never actually let them have fun. I always forget that I'm supposed to let them have fun.

As a reader, who are some of your favorites?

I love the work of Samuel Delany, including his writing about writing. I think his work helps me understand conceptual questions behind writing and behind the politics of any particular fictional world. But I don't try to emulate his writing—A., that would be impossible, and B., it's not who I am as a writer.

Then there's William Vollmann. I don't know that we have similar political outlooks, but I'm intrigued by his writing on the level of, say, sentence structure. And I'm a fan of how Thomas Pynchon uses weather, even though I was just reading Elmore Leonard's *10 Rules for Good Writing* and the first rule is *Never open a book with weather*. But actually if you look at how much Pynchon uses weather, it's very somatic. He'll be describing something, and then, to move you in time and place, he'll focus the narrative eye on the weather, describe it—and then you'll be somewhere else. And I really love thrillers. Philip Kerr. Tana French. Lots more.

How do you know when you've come across a story or historical character that fascinates you enough to devote a book to? Like Jack Sheppard[1]?

I was working on certain questions about the birth of certain kinds of modern forms of gendered embodiment and the intersection of those forms with the rise of British imperialism and the development of the prison system. So, I think that type of question was just bound to hold my attention. But it takes a serious act of will to commit to writing a novel. I worked on *Confessions* for like a couple years and then both my parents died. I put it down for a couple years and I didn't know that I would go back to it. But I remember being about to turn forty-five, and thinking, *I'm a very anxious person who doesn't believe in or trust anything.* So I just thought of writing this novel as an experiment for my forty-fifth birthday—I said, *I'm just going to decide to believe that I can write this book and I'll spend a year believing it. And, if at the end of the year, I don't get anywhere—then I'll put it away and won't write.*[2]

That's a great jacket, by the way.[3]

I got it from eBay, but yes, it is a very nice jacket—thanks. Having been raised by a yenta, clothes are an extremely guilty pleasure. I have to fight my absolute ravenousness around clothing. Which relates to how we lived when I was growing up. We had a rent-controlled apartment. My sister and I shared a bedroom until I went to college. The apartment was not kept up. My parents never bought furniture. That generation just inherited

---

1   The notorious eighteenth-century London thief-lover at the center of *Confessions of the Fox.*

2   Clearly, his experiment worked. *Confessions of the Fox* was published by One World in 2018 to much acclaim.

3   Not the book jacket, the very stylish leather jacket that Jordy was wearing. Yes, it's a total non-sequitur.

some furniture and that was the furniture. So the couch was forty years old and didn't fit anybody. It just kept getting re-slipcovered, right? But the couch was not even functional. The house wasn't a place for show. It was all about the body, and it was all about clothing.

On 9/11, I was trapped with my mother in that apartment. I was living in Brooklyn, and I'd gone to my mother's to pick up my sister to drive her to JFK. She was flying to California that day. So we were there, and then the attacks happened and then they closed the bridges. I had my dog. We couldn't get home. My mother and I were at each other's throats. But we're all stuck there in the apartment.

The next day, or maybe September 13th, my mother was back at Bloomingdale's the minute they reopened its doors. She *had* to go to Bloomingdale's. I know that feeling and have to really fight it. That's my very guilty pleasure—clothes.

Could be a lot worse.

Yes, it could.

Golden Girl

JOHN KUNTZ

(Lights up on a woman in evening wear, seated. There is a martini glass and shaker on a small table next to her chair. She laughs and speaks to an unseen man seated across from her.)

CAN I GET YOU ANOTHER MARTINI, STAN?
(Pause) Yes, maybe we had better. I'm going to have a terrible hangover in the morning. *(Pause)* So. Thank you for seeing me home tonight, Stan. You're a real gentleman. I'm sorry. I'm a little rusty at all this. I haven't been on a date in a very long time. *(Pause)* 30 years. Well, that's very flattering Stan, but I'm a little older than you might think. I'm 62. Well, thank you. Coconut Cream. *(Pause)*. Coconut Cream. That's my secret. It keeps my skin young and wrinkle-free. It was something I learned when I ... Well, never mind. *(Pause)* I think I will have another martini, if you don't mind, Stan. *(Makes martini)* I like to have about 5 martinis before I go to bed.

I know what you're thinking. You're thinking: "Red light. This girl's got a problem." Correction: This *woman's* got a problem.

You see, 30 years ago, I was a nightclub singer and a hopeful actress. Oh, I had appeared in a few films but the reviews hadn't been kind. I played the Leech woman in "Revenge of the Leech Woman," but the critics kept comparing me to the original Leech woman, who possessed an inner flame of Vesuvian proportions.

Apparently you can't warm fondue over my inner flame.

I also played a mangled corpse that gets washed up on shore during the opening credits of "Beach of Doom." It was some of my best work. It was during the filming of "Beach of Doom" that I met Tony. Tony said he recognized me from "Revenge of the Leech Woman." I didn't know whether to be flattered or insulted, since you can't see my face, or really, any part of my body once I had the Leech costume on, which, in that particular film, was all the time. Tony said he had seen "Revenge of the Leech Woman" 5 times and thought it was better than the original and that my work had been really great. He said he had met Barbara Sue Perkins—the original Leech Woman—at a Malibu party and that she was a cunt. I said: "I can't believe you just said that word to me." Tony said I better get used to hearing that word in this business and we left it at that.

I was attracted to and repelled by Tony at the same time, and that can be kind of fascinating. He was handsome in a big, broken sort of way. Tony's two front teeth were missing and replaced with gold ones. He said he was going to be my manager from now on and that he'd make me a star ... a real star ... the star I was meant to be ... He said everything he touched turned to gold and he tapped his front teeth and gave a Midas grin, like a rabid, metallic Cheshire cat and he said that when he touched me I'd turn to gold ... a golden girl.

And then he said we should fuck. I said: "I can't believe you just said that to me!" And then we fucked. It was alright, I guess. I had never made love to anyone before. I thought it would be a wondrous, special thing. I thought it would feel like the wings of a thousand hummingbirds brushing over my skin. I thought I would hear a million bells ringing at once. I thought I would see all the stars in the galaxy parade by me. And I did. But not in the way you might think. I heard bells and saw stars when Tony hit me. He hit me so hard he dislocated my jaw. Luckily, when he hit me again, he knocked it back into place. I hadn't meant to make him mad.

When Tony took off his clothes, I had expected that everything would be ... proportional. Tony was a big man. But his penis was actually tiny. It looked like one of those little cocktail wieners. Only smaller. And then Tony said: "Well? What do you think?" And I said: "Hey. I ate about 10 of those last night on a toothpick!" That's when he hit me.

Tony said he was real sorry about my jaw the next day. He brought me flowers and a heart-shaped box of chocolates. He said if I ever tried to leave him he would kill me. I said: "Oh, Tony. You're so romantic." We flew to Hawaii the next day. Tony had booked me a job singing at a cocktail lounge in Honolulu called the "Wicky Wacky Hula Hut." (*She laughs to herself.*) Sorry. That name still makes me laugh. Honolulu. One night, before the show, I walked into Tony's office at the club and there was a briefcase on his desk filled with bags of white powder ... it looked like flour. I thought maybe Tony was going to bake a cake.

Later, I was right in the middle of singing "I Wanna Be Loved by You" when it hit me like a sack of potatoes: That wasn't flour. It was some kind of drug. Tony was selling drugs, probably illegally. When I realized what was really happening I just stopped singing and walked off the stage. Tony grabbed me. "Where do you think you're going?" he snarled. I said: "I'm gettin' out of here, Tony. I wasn't born yesterday you know. I can't get mixed up in this!" And he said "You can't leave now, you'll blow our cover. Now get out there and sing!"

I took a deep breath and then I said: "I'd tell you to go fuck yourself but with your dick that would be impossible." And then I ducked, which was smart because Tony's fist missed my face and got stuck in the wall behind me. It gave me time to run out of the club and onto the pier. I didn't know where to go. I was wearing a white evening gown with sequins and people were staring at me. I started off towards the end of the pier, where it was dark and there were fewer people. I don't know. At the time, I thought that was a good idea.

Tony caught me halfway down the pier. He grabbed me by the shoulders and began shaking me. I said: "Tony, let me go. I can't do this. I can't be some gangsters' girlfriend. I have to go back to Hollywood. I'm going to be a star. I have talent." "Talent?" He laughed. "You're nothing but a pair of tits with red hair!"

And then he hit me. His diamond-studded horseshoe pinkie ring cut my lip and I fell onto the planked floor of the pier. "Tony," I said "You promised you wouldn't hit me again." "Yeah?" He said. "Well, I guess I lied." And then I saw him raise his fist, the horseshoe glimmering in the moonlight.

I didn't know what to do. I was frantic. As he came toward me I took off my shoe and I shut my eyes and hit Tony in the face. There was this awful silence. I waited for Tony to hit me, but he didn't. When I opened my eyes, Tony was standing in front of me, like a statue, perfectly still, like he had turned to gold. My shoe was hanging off his face. The spike heel had gone right though his eye. Tony had this look on his face I had never seen before. He looked so lost and defeated with that shoe on his face. And then he fell on his knees and slumped over on his side. I knew he was dead. I had to get out of there.

I grabbed my shoe off Tony's face. It made this horrible sucking noise and his eyeball came out on the heel. I put on my shoe, which was now exhibit A, I guess, and ran down the pier. There was a little boat leaving the dock and I jumped aboard just as they were taking the gang plank in. Sightseeing. Whale watching. Something like that. All I cared about was that it would take me away, get me away from my life, from Tony, from everything. When no one was looking, I took Tony's eyeball off my heel and threw it overboard. I watched as an errant, passing porpoise swallowed it like a gumball, and I knew that my love affair with Tony was over.

(She regards her olive, then eats it)

I must have blacked out. When I opened my eyes a handsome man smiled. I thought I was in heaven. "Where am I?" I asked, "What happened?" As he helped me stand up, the handsome man said, "Don't you remember? There was a horrible storm. We were almost drowned, but luckily, we washed up on this beach. My name is Professor Roy Hinkley."

"It's nice to meet you, Professor."

And then I told him my name: "Ginger. Ginger Grant."

Soon I met the other survivors of the wreck. There was the Skipper and his first mate, Gilligan. A wealthy couple named the Howells, and a pretty, pig-tailed girl named Mary Ann. *(Pause. Wistfully.)* Mary Ann ... *(She drinks)* We soon discovered that we were on an uncharted desert island. I know that sounds impossible but what can you do? I'm sure, you recognize me now, Stan: our rescue after 30 years was in all the papers. I would like to say though, that when the Howells died 15 years after the wreck, of natural causes—we did not eat them, as the tabloids claim. But I have to admit: the thought did cross our minds. You get so sick of coconuts after a while.

I know this is an awful lot to lay on you on a first date, Stan, but I like you, and I want this to work out.

Life on the island wasn't really all that bad. The Professor designed really quite elaborate huts for us all to live in. In the 30 years we were there, he built a battery recharger out of coconuts, a bamboo telescope, a Geiger counter, a washing machine, a water pump, a telegraph, lead radiation suits and a pedal-powered bamboo sewing machine. It's funny, with all that, he still couldn't build a boat. Still, I think the Professor really was a genius. He knew so much. Sometimes I thought he even knew about Tony. But I never told him. I never told anyone. Not until tonight.

(Pause. Making a drink, changing subject)

After the Howells Bar-BQ, I mean funeral, the Skipper and Gilligan formally announced that they were lovers. It really was no surprise. We would often hear their groans from their hut late at night: "Oh, Skipper .... Oh, little buddy ... Oh, Skipper ... Oh, little buddy." Really, I'm not sure when they ever slept. I never saw two people who loved each other more. Gilligan caught a horrible tropical disease a few years after the wreck. The Professor tried everything he could to save him, but it was no use. When he died, the Skipper took Gilligan's body up in his arms and he climbed up the little peak on the island ... and he jumped right into the volcano. I guess he just couldn't bear the thought of living without Gilligan. None of us could, really. We even called the island "Gilligan's Island" because he seemed so much a part of it.

For the next 10 years or so, until that ship finally found us, it was just me, the Professor, and Mary Ann. One night, HA!, one crazy night ... the three of us got drunk on some home-made hooch the Professor had distilled from tree sap and pineapple cores and 20 years of sexual repression exploded in a frenzy. Suddenly we were just tearing the clothes off each other, kissing and squeezing and caressing; smearing Mary Ann's coconut cream pie all over our bodies and then licking it off. I threw Mary Ann's gingham dress up in a palm tree. "You won't be needing this anymore!" I hiccuped. The Professor bit my butt. I have never been so sexually overwhelmed in my whole life. To one side of me, the Professor, all hardness and logic and a tongue like a motor boat. And to the other side of me, Mary Ann, so soft and supple, her hands washing over my body like warm milk, her corn-fed, tawny limbs and gravity-defying breasts entwining around my pale, inexperienced ones ... they pressed their bodies against mine, it was a Ginger sandwich ... and then they dived down between my legs like drunken pearl divers, their tongues as precise as clockmaker's screwdrivers ... and when I climaxed, I heard a million bells ringing at once, and the wings of a thousand hummingbirds brushed over my skin, and all the stars in the galaxy danced over me. Just like I knew they would. And that night I knew I was in love ... with the Professor ... and Mary Ann. We were together, like that, for a long time.

And one night, while the Professor and Mary Ann were off gathering coconuts, and I was waiting for them to come back to me, I realized that I was happy. For the first time in my life, I was happy. I had forgotten about Tony, and Hollywood, and fame. I was in love and I was loved in return, and I didn't need anything else. And that's when I saw the ship. Just a dot on the horizon. And I knew that it was coming to take us away. That we were going to be saved .... *(pause)*

Things had changed a lot since we were away. I found out that no one even suspected that I was responsible for Tony's death. The police assumed it had been a bizarre Mob hit and closed the case long ago. When we got back to Honolulu, *(she smiles briefly)* Mary Ann flew back to her family in Kansas. We said good-bye at the airport and I told her I would visit soon. But I knew things would never be the same. The Professor resumed his studies of tropical ferns at the University of Hawaii. When I went to visit him after one of his lectures, he shook my hand. And I knew that whatever door had opened inside him on the island was closed forever. Meanwhile, I had earned a lot of money while I was gone from the residuals for "Revenge of the Leech Woman." It had turned into a cult classic, evidently.

When I got back to Hollywood a Producer called me right away about doing a TV remake. He thought I could re-introduce the Leech Woman to a whole new generation of viewers. And, of course, the public was dying to see Ginger Grant after a 30-year exile. Soon, offers were pouring in left and right. I was going to be a star after all. After all this time, my dream was finally going to come true. And I realized that it meant nothing. It meant absolutely nothing. And do you know what I did? I turned it all down, I tore the phone out of the wall, I told them all to go to hell. I didn't want to be a star anymore.

I wanted to be rescued.

I wanted to be saved.

You see, I'm still waiting for someone to save me from ... all this. Maybe you're the one, Stan. Will you save me? Will you? *(Pause. Ginger makes herself another drink. She begins to sing softly:)* I wanna be loved by you ... Just you. And nobody else but you. I wanna be loved by you. Alone ...

(The lights have faded out.)

Date Night

DAN GROTE

THEY SAY PRISON PRESERVES A GUY, and I guess it does. I'm the same insecure asshole I was when I went in six years ago. Two thousand one hundred and eighty-nine nights, dreaming of this, my first meal of free-people's food. Seventy-two months of penitentiary fare makes even this Hooters' knock-off of a sports bar seem like Morton's.

I didn't pick the place, Corey did. I guess she figured a healthy, red-blooded misanthrope such as myself would appreciate tits and ass with my beer and burger. She's right and I make no apologies. You'd be hard-pressed to find a more unlikely friendship, our equation being one in which none of the variables should provide a solution. She, a self-described "polyamorous queer," who could quote Subcomandante Marcos, Bhanu Kapil, and the Flying Burrito Brothers. Myself, a twice-convicted, perpetually horny, new ex-con with a quick and profane tongue, who could quote Sam Kinison, Doug Stanhope, and a line or two from most every limerick known to man. She, who was militantly against the objectification of all the female species. And me, a sucker for anything with a rack and a pulse.

Something happened to me in prison (not *that* . . .). I went from writing suicide notes read by no one to writing poetry and prose read by the few people who still read literary journals. She was serving her term as editor-in-chief of one of those new lit mags that promised social justice and the avant-garde. A submission from me produced a rejection from her, which contained enough inquisitiveness, encouragement, and opportunity for future dialogue to turn into a regular correspondence. A correspondence that birthed, in my fractured mind, one of the most unusual, yet ultimately fulfilling non-sexual couplings since the Reese family's shotgun wedding of chocolate and peanut butter.

My name's Russell—after a father who stuck around just long enough to give me his name and a royal flush of addiction genes—but everyone calls me Magoo. Out of all the things I could've picked up in prison, a shitty nickname's probably not the worst. Quite frankly, I don't get it. I look much more like an alcoholic/psychopathic truck driver than I do an old, blind cartoon character.

"You're shorter than I'd pictured," Corey says.

"Yep, it's always that way, it seems," I say.

"I'm thinking the grouper sandwich, but I hope it's caught according to Greenpeace's fair catch standards."

I'm not sure I hear her correctly, nor do I have any clue what constitutes a fair catch in her, Greenpeace's, or the fish's mind—I guess I'm not really listening. It's not that I don't want to, it's just that my years *inside* aren't letting me. I'm like a dog that's been at the pound too long and finally found a home. I'm skittish, aloof. Wary and distant. I like where I am right now. I'm just not used to it.

"Don't you loathe commercial fishing?" she asks.

Here's where I should point out, once again, that Corey's everything that I'm not. I care deeply about how my food tastes. However, I could not give less of a shit about how the fish is caught, the cows are killed, the chickens are plucked, or the turkeys are stuffed. I want delicious, free-world food, and I don't care who is exploited in the process. I am, for all intents and purposes, still a bad person. Alcoholic? Check. Drug addict? Absolutely. Misogynist? Not even sure what that means, exactly, but it's very possible. Raised by white trash and left to my own

devices since the age of seventeen, it's a wonder I'm not rot-
ting on Death Row.

"I think I'll go with the veal cutlet sandwich."

"Russ, do you know what veal is made of?" The look of pitiful disdain she gives me while asking this question is only a
shade less severe than the one my answer earns.

"Sure, it's made of meat."

"Baby cows, Russ. Little. Innocent. Baby. Cows."

I can tell she wants to continue her tirade, but I manage to
cut her off. "You know what, Corey, you're right. What do you
want me to say? *I'm sorry? I'm a piece of shit who eats meat?* Old
habits die hard." I'm an old pro at apologizing for my actions,
even if I don't mean it.

"What about the linguine with clams, Corey? Clams don't
have feelings, do they?"

The look I get now is akin to the one the two-year-old who
just shit in the sandbox will receive from his peers.

"Russell, clams are one of the most exploited mollusks
and—"

I interrupt her, "How about you order for us?"

The relief on both sides of the table is palpable. She looks
more than a bit smug that it's taken me less than ten minutes
to concede my first post-lockup meal to her whimsy.

"I need to take a leak, I mean, use the restroom." My sudden attempt at manners catches us both off guard, and I get
up and try my best not to look like I don't want to come back.

At first glance, the bathroom looks only a hair north of san-
itary, like one found 'round back of a decrepit Texaco station.
That I didn't need a key tethered to a hubcap or part of an
engine block is only a slight consolation. I splash some water
on my face and look purposefully into a cracked mirror, talking
to my reflection as if it might be someone who cared.

"What the fuck are you doing here, Magoo?"

The last time I had any kind of in-depth conversation with
the Man in the Mirror was the day before I knocked over my

last bank. It was in a gas station crapper, and I was getting ready to use some toilet water to shoot up the last of my speed. The sink wasn't working and, well, desperate times call for desperate measures. If memory serves, at that time I was trying to convince my reflection that I still had my shit together. Seriously, though. What the hell *am* I doing here? Me, in here, wishing I had some dope. And her, out there, wishing everything once alive on the menu had died of natural causes.

Actually, I do have some dope, just not the kind I'd prefer. I've got an eightball of coke in my pocket that I've been carrying around since yesterday. I was mostly sober the whole time I was locked up. Historically, though, it's always just a matter of time—and not much time, mind you—until I throw it all away. Seems to me that now's as good a time as any. A bump or two might make this evening sufferable.

I fish the baggie out of my pocket—sure doesn't look like much. Time stands still, and when I finally snap back from wherever I went, I'm washing my hands in a dirty sink, with no idea why I just flushed some really good fishscale down the toilet. Turns out a blackout, even a short one, is a hell of a lot more confusing when you're sober.

Whatever it is, something steers me back to the table, and once again, here we are, across from each other. Drinks have materialized since I was away, and Corey sits solemnly, sipping hers like a bird. I down my soda in one smooth, purposeful gulp and look up to see her eyeing me warily.

"Thank you," I say. "Was kinda hoping for something a bit stronger, but all the same, haven't had a Coke in years."

"So did you know that the Coca-Cola Company has a long history of—"

"Stop, Corey! *Please*, just stop. I just got rid of a bunch of coke and—"

"I know," she says, "Just watched you. You must've been thirsty, you—"

"NO, Corey, damn it. Cocaine. I just flushed a whole sack of powder down the shitter. Coke that I bought. Coke that I really wanted to use. The bathroom in this dump is something else, by the way. Oh, and before you say it, I'm sure the coca leaves used to make said blow were harvested by mistreated Colombian peasant folk, so save me the lecture. I flushed it. It's gone. End of story."

My outburst doesn't seem to faze my dinner companion, but a passing busboy looks concerned. Corey looks like she had expected this whole scene.

"Why?" she asks.

"Why *what*? Why? That's the problem. I don't know. I don't know anything. I don't know why I'm here. I don't know why you're here, I—"

"I'm here because we're friends, Russell."

"And?"

"And nothing. That's it. We're friends. Don't ask why. Don't ask how. We just are. I'm happy about that. I'm happy you're out of the stir. I'm happy we're here. And I'm happy you didn't use your drugs."

"Stir?" I laugh. "*Stir*? What the fuck is this, a 1930s' crime drama. Stir?"

"Russ, I just—"

"I'm sorry, Corey. I'm glad we're friends, too. Look at me, though. I'm a mess. And we couldn't be more different. It's just confusing to me. You don't need this. I'm fresh out of the joint and already having trouble keeping it together. I was gonna get high."

"But you didn't, did you?"

"No. You're not mad?"

"Now? No. If you did it, probably."

"But ten minutes ago you were all in my shit about what I was gonna eat. I—"

"I wasn't all *in your shit*. I wasn't yelling and I wasn't lecturing. I was telling you something you might not have known, something I thought you *should* know."

She pauses for a second. "Look, this is awkward for both of us. We're different. But we're fucked up in the same way. In one of your first letters, you told me you were, and I quote, *much better with your pencil than your tongue*. Now, we both know you were referring to being more comfortable dealing with life by writing about it than talking. We also know you were being horny and suggestive with your double entendre, which I found endearing."

I smiled.

"To a point."

My smile faded.

"You also said, sometime later, that you felt like a fraud and that you were hiding behind the words you wrote. You've had a handful of stories and poems published, and in every single one of them you're not hiding a damn thing. You're hanging yourself out for everyone to see, with every sentence. The you I know, the true you? That's what comes out, that's what people like. So this whole *shy man-child hiding behind the chicken-scratch you call writing* charade? It's bullshit."

I've got to admit, the dig on my penmanship hurt.

"You're not a bad person, Russ. You've made mistakes. I've made mistakes. It's up to us, and shame on us if we repeat them. Face it, we're both damaged goods. Everyone is."

"So what're you saying?"

"Nothing. That's the point. Without our pasts, neither of us would be sitting here. So let's just enjoy it."

Our food arrives. Hers looks like a botanical garden on a plate. Mine, well, mine, by God, is an enormous slab of what used to be a cow.

"You got me a *steak*?"

"Look," Corey says. "You are who you are. I am who I am. For what it's worth, it works. In letters and in person. Right here, right now—it works. Sometimes it's not about how different the pieces are. It's about how they fit together. How they complement each other."

She's right. Corey's the first friend I've had in a long time. The first female friend I've ever had that I haven't tried to talk into bed. She's as granola as can be, and goddamnit, she's got me pegged. I get the waitress's attention, making no apologies for ogling her ample chest, and hear Corey laugh as I ask for a splash of bourbon in my refill.

I look across the table and smile at her as she cuts her lettuce or watercress or whatever the fuck it is. I slice into my ribeye with no empathy whatsoever and chew, savoring my freedom, thinking about this friendship, and waiting, eagerly, for Corey to tell me something else she thinks I should know.

The Art of Getting to the Point

WESLEY BROWN

IN 1981, TONI CADE BAMBARA RECEIVED (along with Paule Marshall and Toni Morrison) the City College of New York's Langston Hughes Award for Lifetime Contributions to African American Arts & Letters. At some point in the program, questions were taken from the audience. A woman asked the honorees why black writers weren't giving their readers more positive stories of black life. Bambara responded immediately, saying, "I've seen you before at literary events, like this one. And you always ask the same question. If there're stories you want to see written, maybe that's your assignment: to write them." This was vintage Bambara, expressing the ethos behind everything she wrote: an unfailing directness, which implicated the reader in the power of language and the responsibilities and consequences that come with using it.

In addition to Bambara's confrontational relationship to language, she possessed the gift for moving quickly to the vital center of a character or dramatic situation. This is immediately apparent when reading the first lines of any of her short stories. For example, "Medley" opens with Sweet Pea who doesn't waste any time getting in our face: "I could tell the minute I got to the door and dropped my bag, I wasn't staying." Sweet Pea has already opened the door and witnessed something before the reader arrives on the scene. We don't know what she sees; but whatever it is, she's ready to vacate the premises. So we're drawn to Sweet Pea's displeasure, not because of any sordid details, but because she has attitude to burn. You would never want to get in her way, but you'd follow her anywhere!

The story "Playin with Punjab," like "Medley," cuts to the 411 on the person we're about to meet: "First of all, you don't play with Punjab." My interest is piqued on the basis of the name alone. It's not the same as "Calvin" or some other moniker unlikely to raise the fear level in the sweat glands. Just the sound: *PUNJAB*. It makes you wince, as though you've just received a blow. Another jarring sensation is delivered in the first line of Bambara's "The Hammer Man": "I was glad to hear that Manny had fallen off the roof." Again, we're not privy to what incited the response of the narrator that would account for her indifference to the calamity suffered by Manny.

Here are more of Bambara's teaser-driven sentences that create expectations, which are almost always fulfilled in her precise and attention-grabbing prose.

Blind people got a hummin' jones if you notice.

That was the year Hunca Bubba changed his name.

The puddle had frozen over and me and Cathy went stompin in it.

In each sentence, the conventional narrative floor, walking us into the story, drops away; and we are sent into a riotous flight of language and storytelling.

My favorite Bambara opening line is from "The Lesson": "Back in the days when everyone was old and stupid or young and foolish and me and Sugar were the only ones just right, this lady moved on our block with nappy hair and proper speech and no make-up." That's quite a load to unpack from the mouth of a sassy, adolescent narrator named Sylvia. From the get-go, Sylvia puts the world on notice that she's peeped on everybody's pedigree, and the reader need go no further to know that her every word and gesture says: I AIN'T HARDLY

IMPRESSED. But despite the finality of Sylvia's judgment of people, the world shows itself to be brain dead as well as pitiful, when an emissary named Miss Moore shows up. For Sylvia, whatever mission brought Miss Moore to the neighborhood is doomed because she belongs to that lowest category of human being known as an adult. All this and more can, legitimately, be read into Bambara's masterful first sentence, which satisfies Edgar Allan Poe's requirement for any story to succeed artistically: to use only those words that are necessary to achieve the intended effect.

So where does Bambara's skill for getting to the point early and often leave us? Do we come away merely dazzled by her virtuosity? These questions are, of course, more than adequately answered by reading the stories that unfold out of her eye opening first lines. But perhaps, the most telling example of Bambara's vision as a writer comes, characteristically enough, from the first line of her novel *The Salt Eaters*, where Minnie Ransom, a legendary spiritual healer asks Velma Henry: "Are you sure, sweetheart, that you want to be well?" Here, Velma Henry is confronted by language that asks her to consider getting well, not as an intervention outside herself, but as an experience in which she is invested with the power to foster or undermine her capacity to heal. Once again, Toni Cade Bambara cuts to the chase and makes the case all in one motion. And that's—point, game, set and match!

Boatbound

CRAIG MOODIE

I GASP AS I WADE INTO THE WATER. Why does it feel so cold today? I suck in my breath and raise my arms as a wave climbs up to my waist. I need to muster the grit to dive in. Why prolong the torture? I go deeper. A wave lifts me off the bottom. When my feet touch sand again, I plunge in before the steep chop splashes over me. One moment I'm stifling an inward scream from the shock, the next I'm surfacing, breaststroking out, my skin adjusting to the chill.

My objective—Finn, our twelve-foot catboat—pitches and rolls on her mooring five hundred feet seaward. Usually my swim to the boat to sail her or bail her out gives me a chance to commune with the substance that floats her. I can exist eye-to-eye with loons and cormorants and terns and gulls. When the tide is low, I can wade the whole way. The water can appear light-filled, airy, a partner in buoyancy. I sidestep samurai crabs, schools of baitfish escorting me through the light-squiggled water.

Not so today. The moon has commanded the tide to reach new heights. The water pushes so high it submerges the jetty and seems intent on swallowing beach and dune. Waves force cold saltwater up my nose. The water is petroleum-dark under the overcast. The wind sends shivers over the waves so that they look as scaly as a sea monster's flanks.

I glance over my shoulder to see my wife sitting on the remaining strip of beach. She looks far from where I set out.

Wind and wave work against me, driving me off course. I've
been pushed slantwise. I breaststroke harder, my arms tiring as
I regain ground. Why do I feel so weak? Has the water drugged
me? Why does the water feel so heavy, so resistant? Now even
my old hole-pocked Top-Siders seem leaden.

I spit out water and sidestroke for a minute. A thought jolts
me: Am I drowning? I speed up my strokes. Halfway out now.
Should I turn around, head back, let the wind and wave gods
carry me where they want me to go? Why did I insist on swimming out instead of taking the dinghy?

I see our boat cutting back and forth on her mooring, buck-
ing and diving. She flashes her stern at me as if urging me on:
You can do it!

I can't let her down. I forge on, the waves steeper now that
I'm farther out. How ridiculous—and possible—drowning in
seven feet of high water could be. And I'm only a couple of
body lengths from the haven of my boat. The grim and embar-
rassing headline: BOATBOUND MAN DROWNS. The thought
propels me onward. I battle closer.

The wind veers, swinging Finn away from me. I kick hard
to close the gap. She swings farther away still. My arms quiver.
A wave slaps my face, closes over my head. The sizzle of the
whitecaps ceases. The water drags me down. I'm going under
fast. Water presses me down, squeezing around me. I drop
deeper, light dissolving.

Then my feet touch solid ... what? I stop sinking, and I drop
my eyes to a form darker than the water just below me—the
form beneath my feet. I see the glow of sandy bottom below
this tubular shape. I'm lifted up, the rubber of my soles gripping the surface of the form. I'm moving forward and up and
then I feel a shove from below delivered by a creature whose
size and power radiate through my body. I'm thrust upward.
I break the surface gagging and my right arm slams against a
solid surface—Finn.

She dips toward me and I grasp her rail. Below me a shadow

as long as our boat undulates by and disappears from view beneath the hull. Icy electricity surges through me as the water swirls as if in a tide race. I haul myself up and over the transom into the cockpit.

My breath comes in heaves at first until I pull myself upright. Soon I feel my pulse easing. I look over the side of the boat: only whitecaps break around us. I raise my eyes beyond them to my wife ashore, a smaller figure now. She lifts an arm and waves. To her I must look the way I always do when I swim out.

I look back over the side, seeing only my wobbling reflection. What did I meet underwater? Was it shark, blackfish, dolphin, seal? Seals were once called dragons. Perhaps it was a sea dragon, or the sea serpent once seen in New England waters making a reappearance from the deeps. Had the extraordinary tide brought it into the shallows? Greenland sharks can live for five hundred years. Why not other creatures that remain unseen to us, ones that make a fortuitous return?

That this one made itself visible is why I remain breathing air as I ride up and down on the deck of our boat. Had it intended to help me? Had it arrived to rescue me by some fluke in the machinations of the aqueous universe, a pelagic beast turned unintentional hero? Or had it meant to devour me but missed?

I go about the business of pumping out the bilge and checking the boat over. Then I climb onto the transom and ready myself to go back in the water. A faint tremble runs through my limbs. I look shoreward to my wife but her gaze lies elsewhere. I pull in a breath and pat the boat's stern. "Time to go back in," I say, and drop my eyes to the dark waters crowding toward me, awaiting my return.

Inventory

(for the poets of Norfolk Correctional Institution)

CHARLES COE

As a child I tried to keep track of certain things: cracks in the sidewalk between the bus stop and school, names of streets between the bridge and our family's house, toy soldiers lined up on a shelf.

Now the list of things I've lost, or forgotten, or thrown away, at times seems longer than the list of what remains. Sometimes this feeling visits uninvited, late at night, when every breath is a footstep measuring the miles till dawn.

But this gray morning as I walked across the yard, the sun suddenly shoved through the clouds to warm my face, and later I was graced by a small kindness from an unexpected source. This is not the life I would have chosen. But I will try to keep an open hand for the gifts it spreads each day across my path, like Easter eggs hidden in the grass.

When the Rains Came

CHARLES COE

Father, I remember that heat wave when after six stifling days and nights we sat together in the front porch shade with a clunky old box fan that gave little relief, with bare feet and bare chests, our raggedy shorts the only nod to modesty.

Then suddenly the sky darkened, a cool breeze ruffled the oak leaves and a trap door opened in the belly of the clouds.

I'd rather not remember you dragging in after your shift at the Chevy plant, making your way from the driveway to the front door slowly, as if bracing yourself for the charged air of that little gray house.

I'd rather remember you on that porch, when we watched in wonder as one thing became another, both of us like children, breathing in together the evanescent smell of cool rain kissing the hot, dry earth.

House Money

CHARLES COE

Two elderly black men navigating the crowded sidewalk on canes stop to greet each other, exchange a handshake complicated as a physics midterm. "Hey man," one exclaims. "I ain't seen you in a dog's age! What's happenin'?"

"Well, I'm still alive," his friend replies, pauses with a comic's timing then adds, "And they still tryin' to kill me."

They laugh and shake their heads in shared awareness, two old black men in America who've beaten the odds.

Now they're playing with house money.

Freaks

BY NIKOLAI GROZNI

IT WAS MORE OR LESS LIKE THIS: the town, a drab, Alpine lair on the Italian-Swiss border, had a long, unmemorable name that started with *C*; the hotel was a mediocre mortuary for seasoned visitors and was run by three generations of short-haired women with glasses; the purpose of my visit had at one point been explained to me by my former wife, but I have since forgotten both the purpose and the name of my former wife, though I'm inclined to think that she and I must've had some children together because, if I remember correctly, when we sat down for breakfast the first morning, there were a few children sitting in the chairs adjacent to us, demanding jam and toast and discussing the surroundings with great impertinence. It was really early in the morning, ten or eleven, and I had just begun to stir the sugar cubes piled up to the rim of my coffee cup, trying to avoid the insolent faces of the children and the ambitiously sculpted wisdoms falling out of my former wife's mouth like death masks, when the French doors swung open and into the dining hall lumbered a large group of circus-rate freaks guided by the wavering wand of a tall, black-cloaked woman with a triangle face whose only claim to normality appeared to be based upon her indisputable possession of a wallet. One by one the freaks sat around a long, apostolic table and started performing their well-rehearsed tricks. My attention was first drawn to a miniature woman with an enormous head, in a polka-dot dress and patent-leather flats, who spoke in a tiny voice and giggled uncontrollably at her own jokes, wrapping her short, baby arms around her head and waggling her legs that barely reached the chair's edge. Noticing that I was looking at her from across the hall, she froze, her eyes distending, and nudged the donkey-headed man sitting next to her, whose primary occupation was to roll his long tongue in and out of his mouth and hee-haw loudly, stretching out his neck to better examine the assembly. Presently, the donkey-headed man noticed me as well and nudged the giant sitting next to him, hee-hawing and pointing at me with what could only be interpreted as great affection. The giant, whose head was caught in the chandelier and whose hands extended across the table, didn't respond right away, and that, admittedly, was quite fitting, since his main concern appeared to center on the exigencies of free will and, in particular, on the initial impulse that sets a scene in motion: there had to be a button, he seemed to think, with his head caught in the chandelier; there had to be a button that pressed the button, and one could not but press, again, the old question regarding causality: which came first, then, the button or the button? The button, I replied in place of the giant, detecting with some annoyance that my disclosure had not failed to elicit a certain flurry of scrutiny on the part of my former wife and the contemptuous children; nor had they failed to notice that I had spilled my coffee and, presently, was pulling the tablecloth and the entire breakfast arrangement onto my lap, owing to the fact that, while attempting to balance the chair on its hind legs, I had inadvertently reached its tipping point and now risked falling backward and smashing my head on the table behind me. The sound of the porcelain teapot shattering on the terrazzo floor attracted the giant's attention and now our eyes met, his and mine, and it was self-evident that I saw myself through his eyes, and he saw himself with my eyes; and whereas I grew instantly attached to his giantness, he grew forthwith attached to my nonexistence,

and as time passed, I felt more and more giant-like, whereas he
felt more and more nonexistent; and had someone asked us, at
that moment, who was the giant and who was the reality hole,
I would've answered that I was the giant, and he would've most
certainly answered that he was the reality hole. He had advanced
so far into the reality hole, in fact, that had he not found in
himself the strength to bend over the hatted lady with one long
and one very short arm sitting to his right and shout in her ear
to look at me, pronto, he would've likely disappeared for good.
But he didn't disappear, and I didn't grow so big as to knock
down the roof of the hotel. I stirred my third cup of coffee with
my pinkie and looked right through my former wife's rather
transparent head, even as she tried to articulate a purely scientific explanation for the somewhat bizarre circumstances that
led to my teaspoon flying into the face of the charming octoge-
narian sitting in the corner of the dining hall. The hatted lady
with one long and one very short arm was winking at me and
demonstrating her ability to drool inordinate amounts of
mouth liquid into the crevice between her giant tits—a feat of
smashing ingenuity that I promised myself to study more
closely in my private quarters at a later time. One of the children had asked me a question, something about midgets or
quantum mechanics, and I answered mechanically, giving my
full attention to the balding bookkeeper with a nose bent
severely to one side who was counting a wad of fake banknotes
and yelling at the hatted lady to stop drooling. I, too, wanted to
count wads of banknotes, fake or otherwise, and distribute
them among the hoi polloi in exchange for a small service fee.
The bookkeeper was well aware of my interest in his machinations and didn't consider it necessary to conceal the sleights of
hand that made his machinations profitable. He looked at me,
I looked at him, and we came to an agreement: I would count
and deal the banknotes using his hands and tongue, taking full
advantage of the legerdemains that he'd perfected after years of

relentless practice; he, on the other hand, would follow my former wife to her private quarters and try to seduce her, using one or more parts of my body and taking full advantage of the nearly metaphysical indifference that she and I exhibited in each other's presence at all times. This, I thought, (getting up, briefly, to dispossess the rather obnoxious individual sitting at the table to my left of his second plate of bacon and toast), was indeed a magnificent proposition, and, loath to delay this matter any further, I nodded to that effect at the bookkeeper, and he nodded back, elbowing the very nervous virtuoso with gray hair sticking up on end, sitting on his right, to take notice of what had taken place and step forward as a reliable witness: which he did, faithfully, pulling his ears, growling like a dog, and smashing his forehead against the table seven times in a row. There was, I noticed now, a lively disagreement underway on the margins of our table involving my former wife, the obnoxious individual, and two of the three short-haired women in charge of the hotel, and, from what I managed to gather with one ear, it appeared that the central premise that the obnoxious individual had put forth revolved around the idea of his preordained and unassailable jurisdiction over his second plate of toast and bacon; whereas my former wife argued that his so-called unassailable jurisdiction over the plate of toast and bacon did not preclude her from having a completely irrelevant and contradictory opinion on the subject, which I thought was a rather weak argument; and as the obnoxious individual took issue with my former wife's argument and then went on to decimate it didactically point by point, I found myself growing increasingly fond of him and made a note in my journal to study his tactics for future use. The disagreement ended suddenly when the red-haired concubine without teeth, who had until then cuddled next to the very nervous virtuoso, climbed onto the table, on the recommendation of the very nervous virtuoso, hiked up her skirt, and sat on top of the chocolate cake

placed before the unseemly fat woman with an alphabet fixa-
tion, thereby drawing a round of applause from all the guests
at the apostolic table who appeared genuinely impressed by
acts of disinhibition and spontaneous regression and turned a
blind eye to the disdainful reaction of other, less inspired
beings. The fact that I, too, was genuinely impressed by the
toothless concubine's cake-smeared buttocks and the subsequent attempt by the bookkeeper to eat the wallet, and then the
entire hand of the black-cloaked lady with the triangle face was
not lost on my former wife and the children; nor, for that matter, did the guests at the apostolic table fail to notice that I
longed to join them and shake off, once and for all, the pre-
tense that I was real and that I understood, wink-wink, the so-
called decorum of existence, whereas I understood absolutely
nothing of the so-called decorum of existence and existed from
day to day by employing acts of trickery and metaphysical acro-
batics that rivaled the creation of the universe, from scratch, or
from a dung beetle, or from the ball of dung pushed by a dung
beetle. For while others appeared to simply exist, abiding effortlessly by the accepted reality, I had to convince everyone around
me that I was one of them and that I also abided effortlessly by
the same reality, even though I couldn't see even the outline of
the so-called reality and merely performed the tasks that had
been described to produce real results, in the hope that everyone would be fooled and I would continue to live among them,
wink-wink, like a wolf among sheep, or a frog among pebbles.
It was undeniable that the whole thing smelled profoundly of
sympathetic magic, spells, and heavy superstition, and I was
tired of pretending that magic spells worked, when in fact they
didn't work at all, or, at best, succeeded in making those
involved miserable in a very real way. I just wasn't one of them,
I thought, noticing how one of the children, maybe a boy,
poured himself another cup of hot chocolate and looked at his
mother with a sense of historic achievement, disregarding the

possibility that both he and his cup of hot chocolate may have existed only as a pair of slippers inside a very brief and insignificant dream dreamed by an ordinary baby maggot attached to the testicles of a leper dog at the Bidhannagar Road rail station in Kolkata. Wink-wink, I winked at the miniature woman with enormous head and tiny voice, who was smiling at me and pushing a plastic straw far up her nose. Wink-wink, she winked back at me, not without a tinge of sadness, for she knew as well as I did that I was rather trapped in my social arrangement and could not join her and her companions just like that, on a whim, lacking advance preparations or at least a few pieces of incontrovertible evidence linking my former wife and the children to the workings of the Gestapo and, before that, by way of metempsychosis, to the illiterate hordes of savages responsible for the sacking of Constantinople. Wink-wink, the very nervous virtuoso winked at me, as he pushed himself away from the table and fell backward in his chair, pounding the terrazzo floor with his reverberant baroque head. They were all leaving now, the freaks, taking their fabulous tricks and vaunts somewhere else, and they were going there without me. I belong with the freaks, I thought, or maybe I even said it out loud, I couldn't tell for certain, and the inscrutable expressions on the faces of the three creatures sitting at my table prevented me from forging a well-informed opinion on the subject. I still had a lot of work ahead of me before I could disengage from the so-called decorum of existence and step lightly across to the other side. Without a doubt, the day would come when I would join the freaks and leave all these drab dolls and their obsessive-compulsive reality rituals behind. I would shake and stick my fingers in my eyes and hop around like a rabbit and bark like a rabid dog. I would walk and sit whichever way I wanted. I would use mixed metaphors and non sequiturs to describe the authorless figment known as reality and achieve nonconceptual love for all living beings, including humans and Meerschaum pipes, by attaching myself to the testicles of a leper dog at the

Bidhannagar Road rail station in Kolkata and surrendering to the spontaneous visions of an uncreated, jalebi-sweetened reverie. Oh, the day would come, the day would certainly come when I would join the freaks and leave all these lies behind. Then, and only then, would I be born for the very first time.

"Freaks" originally appeared as the first chapter of *Claustrophobias*, published by Begemot in Bulgaria.

Boston Marriage

PAGAN KENNEDY

LIZ IS EXPLAINING THE SITUATION to some guy in customer service. "My roommate and I need to network our computers together," she's saying, seated at the other desk in the office that we share.

The word "roommate" jumps out at me. It's an inadequate word, but it's all we have. What else do you call two friends who are shacked up together in a decaying Victorian, run several businesses and one nonprofit group out of its rooms, host political meetings under oil portraits of Puritan and Jewish ancestors, cook kale and tofu meals for all who stop by, go to parties as a couple, and spend holidays with each other's families? If we were lesbians—as people sometimes assume us to be—we would fit more neatly into a box. But we're straight.

In the year and a half we've lived together, I have struggled with the namelessness of our situation. The word "roommate" conjures up a college dorm, scuff marks on the floors from hundreds of anonymous occupants, locks on all the doors, the refrigerator Balkanized into zones where you can or cannot put your food, death metal blasting from the speakers down the hall. It means transience and twenty years old. It does not mean love or family.

Words offer shelter. They help love stay. I wish for a word that two friends could live inside, like a shingled house with faded Persian rugs. Sometimes, in an attempt to make our relationship sound more valid, I tell people Liz and I are in a "Boston marriage." The usual response is "You're in a what?"

It's an antique phrase, dating back to the 1800s. In Victorian times, women who wanted to maintain their independence and freedom opted out of marriage and often paired up to live together, acting as each other's "wives" and "helpmeets." Henry James's 1886 novel about such a liaison, *The Bostonians,* may have been the inspiration for the term, or perhaps it was the most glamorous female couples who made their homes in Boston, including Sarah Orne Jewett, a novelist, and her "wife" Annie Adams Fields, also a writer.

Were they gay? Was "Boston marriage" simply code for lesbian love? The historian Lillian Faderman says this is impossible to determine, because nineteenth-century women who kept diaries drew curtains over their bedroom windows. They did not bother to mention whether their ecstatic friendship spilled over into—as Faderman so romantically puts it—"genital sex." And ladies, especially well-to-do ones who poured tea with their pinkies raised, were presumed to have no sex drive at all. Women could share a bed, nuzzle in public, and make eyes at each other, and these cooings were considered to be as innocent as schoolgirl crushes.

So, at least in theory, the Boston marriage indicated a platonic, albeit nerdy relationship. With ink-stained fingers, the Victorian roommate-friends would smear jam on thick slices of bread and then lounge across from each other in bohemian-shabby leather armchairs to discuss a novel-in-progress or a political speech they'd just drafted. Their brains beat as passionately as their hearts. The arrangement often became less a marriage than a commune of two, complete with a political agenda and lesson plan.

"We will work at [learning German] together—we will study everything," proposes Olive, a character in *The Bostonians,* to her ladylove. Olive imagines them enjoying "still winter evenings under the lamp, with falling snow outside, and tea on a little table, and successful renderings . . . of Goethe, almost the only foreign author she cared about; for she hated the writing of the French, in spite of the importance they have given to women." James poked fun at Olive's bookworm passion. But he lavished praise on his own sister Alice's intense and committed friendship with another woman, which he considered to be pure, a perfect devotion.

Most likely, the Boston marriage was many things to many women: business partnership, artistic collaboration, lesbian romance. And sometimes it was a friendship nurtured with all the care that we usually squander on our mates—a friendship as it could be if we made it the center of our lives.

"I am on my way through the green lane to meet you, and my heart goes scampering so, that I have much ado to bring it back again, and learn it to be patient, till that dear Susie comes," Emily Dickinson wrote to her friend—and maybe lover—Sue Gilbert. Today I see tragedy in these words, for Sue ended up married to Emily's brother, and the women never had a chance to build a life around their love. I find myself wishing I could teleport them to our own time, so that Emily D. and her Susie might find an apartment in San Francisco together, fly a rainbow flag out front, shop at Good Vibrations, and delight each other with dildos in shocking shades of pink. And yet, it's not that simple. When I read the passionate letters between nineteenth-century women, I become keenly aware of what I'm missing, of how much richer Victorian friendships must have been. While our sex lives have ballooned in the last hundred years, our friendships have grown stunted. Why don't I shower my favorite girls with kisses and mash notes, hold hands with them as we skip down the street, or share a sleeping bag? We don't touch anymore. We don't dare admit how our hearts scamper.

Several years ago, I fell in love with a man because of all he carried—he would show up for the night with five plastic bags rattling on his arm, and then proceed to unpack, strewing possessions everywhere. The next day, I'd find his orange juice in the refrigerator, his sweater tucked into my bureau, a software program installed on my computer. Night after night, he installed himself in my apartment.

At first, every one of these discoveries charmed me—his way of saying, "I need to be with you." But one morning I surveyed my bedroom—guy's underwear on the floor, books about artificial intelligence stacked on the night table, a jar of protein powder on the shelf—and realized that I had a live-in boyfriend. And that he and I had completely different ideas about what we wanted from a living space. He thought of an apartment as a desktop where we could scatter papers, coffee mugs, and computer parts. What I regarded as a mess, he saw as a filing system that should under no circumstances be disturbed. Meanwhile, I drove him crazy by hosting political meetings in our living room, inviting ten people over for dinner at the last minute. We loved each other, but that didn't mean we should share an apartment.

And then, when our Felix-Oscar dynamic seemed insurmountable, I picked up a magazine called *Maxine* and stumbled across an article that gripped me. Written by twenty-seven-year-old Zoe Zolbrod, it celebrated the passion that flashes up between women, even when they are both straight. "I would meet women who I would need to know with an urgency so crushing it gave the crush its name. And in knowing them I would feel a rush of power and possibility, of total self, that seemed much more real to me than heterolove," Zolbrod wrote. When she met her friend V, "it was like finding the person you think you'll marry." The two moved in together. They took care of each other, became family, called each other "my love" and "my roommate" interchangeably.

I remember reading that article and thinking, "Yes." I adored my boyfriend, but he and I had never meshed in the way that Zolbrod described. We tried to make a home together, but we didn't agree on what a home should be.

Years later, when our love fizzled into friendship and he moved out, I made a vow to myself: I would not drift into a domestic situation again. Instead, I would find someone who shared my passion for turning a house into a community center—with expansive meals, weekend guests, clean counters, flowers, art projects, activist gatherings, a backyard garden, and a pile of old bikes on the porch, available to anyone needing to borrow some wheels.

My friend Liz seemed like the right person. And so I proposed to her. Did she want to be a cocreator of the performance art piece that we would call "home"? She did.

Recently, at a party, I met a thirty-something academic who has settled alone in a small town outside Boston. "I can step right out my door and cross-country ski," she told me. "But I'm lonely a lot." Around us, people sweated and threw their arms wildly in time to an old Prince song. The academic wedged her hands into her jeans pockets, and her eyes skated past my face and scanned the room.

If you're lonely, get a roommate, I suggested. Move into a group house. "No," she said, sighing. "I'm too old for that. I'm set in my ways." What if you marry? I asked. She laughed. "That's different."

She might be speaking for thousands, millions of women all over this country. According to the U.S. Census Bureau, one out of four households in 1995 had only one member, a figure expected to rise as the population ages. I see the future of single women, and frankly, it depresses the hell out of me. We're isolating ourselves in condos and studio apartments. And why? Sometimes because we need to bask in solitude—and that's fine. But other times, it's because we're afraid to get too comfortable with our friends. What if you bought a house with your best friend, opened a joint bank account with her, raised a child? Where would your bedmate fit into the scheme? This is where the platonic marriage—for all its loveliness—may force you to make some difficult choices and rethink your ideas about commitment.

Liz's love, a theoretical physicist, meanders down our street clapping. Standing beside a triple-decker house, he cocks his head, listening to the sharp sounds reverberating off a vinyl-sided wall. He's designing an exercise for the students in the Physics of Music class that he's assistant-teaching. When he's done, he'll come back inside to find Liz and me draped across the sofa, discussing urban sprawl. We'll all make dinner together, and if I feel like it, I might join them for a night out, or I might head off with the guy I'm seeing.

I date scientists too, men who understand what it is to experiment, to question and wonder. Liz's love or mine might sit in our kitchen scrawling equations into a notebook, or disappear for days to orbit with subatomic particles or speak with machines. These men are wise enough to see that the Boston marriage works to their advantage. Liz and I keep each other company. Our Boston marriage has made it easier for us to enjoy the men in our lives.

But how do we commit to each other, knowing that someday one of us may marry? One of us might fall in love with something other than a man—a solar cabin in Mexico, a job in Tangier, a documentary film project in Florida, a year of silence in the Berkshire woods. Any number of things could pull us apart. We have made no promises to each other, signed no agreements to commit. For some reason, that seems OK most of the time.

For this piece, I talked to many women who'd formed platonic marriages or who'd thought about it seriously. All of them discussed the complicated issue of commitment, or lack thereof, between friends.

Janet calls her arrangement with Greta intentional. "In the same vein as creating an 'intentional community,' we have an 'intentional' living arrangement," she says. The two high school friends, both straight women in their early thirties, moved to

Boston together five years ago, knowing that they would share an apartment, and a life. They eat dinner together and check in with the how-was-your-day conversation most people expect from a mate.

"Greta is the person I say to contact when I fill out emergency cards," Janet tells me. "She is the first person I would turn to if I needed help."

And yet the two have left their future open, and the promises they have made to each other are full of what-ifs. If Greta doesn't marry by the time she's thirty-five, they might raise a child together. It's the what-ifs that drive many women away from closeness with each other.

One married woman, I'll call her Lisa, says she's deeply disappointed with the way women treat their friendships as disposable, dumping friends when an erotic partner comes along. "Even though my friends and I used to talk about buying a house together, we all knew at some level that it wasn't going to work. Ultimately, we would betray each other, find a man, marry him. I got married because I knew everybody else was going to. If I knew I could trust a friendship with a woman— that there was a way of making a friendship into a bona fide, future-oriented relationship—I would rather have that than be married."

As for me, I've come to think of commitment as something beyond a marriage contract, a joint bank account, or even a shared child. I know that eventually Liz and I may drift to other houses, other cities. Yet I can picture us reuniting at age eighty, to settle down in an old-age home together. Maybe we will have husbands, maybe not, but we'll still be conspirators. We'll probably harangue the youngsters who spoon spinach onto our plates about the importance of forming a union; we'll attend protests with signs duct-taped to our walkers; maybe we'll write an opera and perform it using some newfangled technology that lets us float in the air. Liz and I are committed. We share a vision of the kind of people we want to be and the world we want to inhabit.

"We formed a family core with the possibility of exhilaration," wrote Zoe Zolbrod in her article. "Yet Hallmark never even named a goddamn holiday after us, can you believe it?" We're not sure what to call ourselves. We have no holidays. We don't know what our future holds. We have only love and the story we are making up together.

Liz sashays into the kitchen, a shopping bag crinkling under her arm. "I bought you these," she says, "because you've been wearing those mismatched gloves with holes in them."

I slide on the mittens, and my hands turn into fuzzy paws, pink and red with a touch of gold. "I love them," I say, and hug her, patting her back with my fuzz. She laughs and shifts her eyes away, a bit embarrassed by her own generosity. "I couldn't have my roommate going around in shabby gloves," she says.

She uses the word "roommate." But I know what she means.

"Boston Marriage" originally appeared *Ms. Magazine* in 2001, and was included in the collection *Our Boston* (Mariner Books).

Postcards

JEFF GORDINIER

As soon as Lauren and I realized that our long-simmering crushes on each other could lead to something serious, I faced a dilemma.

She was moving to Los Angeles a week later. I lived north of New York City, and I needed to stay put for a few years in order to be present for my two school-age children, who lived with their mother most of the time. How were Lauren and I going to make this last?

I knew enough about my own history and the predictable trajectories of long-distance relationships to realize that a romance dependent on and nurtured by technology—texts, emails, selfies, obligatory FaceTime sessions with unfortunate close-ups of my neck—would probably peter out in spasms of frustration. I needed another approach.

That's when I started sending Lauren postcards. Hundreds of postcards, enough to fill a couple of shoe boxes, over the course of a year. (I had been a passionate postcard aficionado in the late 1980s and early 1990s, as a way of staying in touch with friends after college, but I'd let the practice lapse.) At her apartment in the Hollywood Hills, Lauren would sometimes receive four or five postcards in a single day. I concede, in retrospect, that this compulsive practice of mine ran the risk of bringing the relationship to a premature end, because it made me look a little overbearing. But postcards, as I have come to learn, have a way of disarming people. Postcards are intrinsically delightful. And they just might be the secret to deepening our connections with the people we care about.

Lauren came to relish the randomness of these deliveries—well, after a period of mild concern. "At first, I thought you were coming on strong with the postcards," she says now. "But I was charmed and had them all on display on my bookshelf. I tried to reciprocate but could not keep up. I started finding myself disappointed when there was a pause, as I became so accustomed to coming home to postcards in the mail."

Lauren never knew what she was going to get next. On any given evening, after coming back from the office, she might find a postcard bearing a portrait of Patti Smith, another graced with the cover of a vintage Italian cookbook, another with a Cézanne still life of apples, another with an image from Vogue from the Roaring Twenties. My work as a food writer can take me all over the world, so on my trips—to Oaxaca and Copenhagen and Seoul, to Houston and Seattle and Memphis—I hoarded local souvenir cards by the dozen. I created an international stockpile of serendipity so that every card Lauren received came as a surprise.

And what did I actually say on the cards? On plenty of them, of course, I would contort myself into fresh ways of telling Lauren that I loved her and missed her. But the objective was not to bombard my girlfriend with effusive declarations; even "I love you" can get a little monotonous if you scribble it on five postcards a day. The objective was just to stay in touch, to keep that element of surprise alive, to let her know she was on my mind, and to do so in a gentle, low-impact way that would subvert the brain-melting frenzy of 21st-century electronic communication instead of contributing to it. So sometimes the postcards carried arbitrary or quotidian observations, two lines of a poem, a song lyric, a snippet from an essay I had just read, a comic sketch of a rude passenger on a plane, gossip, mantras, complaints, recipes, childhood memories, descriptions of weather.

Through falling in love with Lauren, it turned out that I fell back in love with postcards too, and I learned that handwritten words on printed paper have a way of strengthening the bonds that social media can feel engineered to erode. I expanded my reach. I started sending out-of-the-blue postcards to my children, Margot and Toby, who are now 16 and 13, and to Ian and Jason and Rosie and Klancy and Pete and other friends. I became a Johnny Appleseed of postal caprice. Instead of seeds, my traveling sack contained stacks of fresh cards: colorful Marimekko designs, paintings by Jean-Michel Basquiat, the Sibley Backyard Birding postcards, the Rad American Women A-Z set, depictions of flowers and fruit from the archives of the New York Botanical Garden, psychedelic posters from the Grateful Dead. Sometimes I would bang out a quick riff referring to the art on the front. But usually I wouldn't. The point wasn't to say anything profound. The point was to express, in a form so compressed that it flirted with haiku, the very core of connectivity: I am thinking of you. I am here, and you are there, but I want to tell you something that just crossed my mind.

People in my life started thanking me. They said they loved receiving the cards through the mail. If an email feels like a burden, a postcard ought to feel like the opposite of a chore—even an antidote. Because of its brevity, a postcard demands very little of its reader, and because the timing of its delivery to the recipient depends on the vicissitudes of the postal service, the whims of weather, and the fickle hand of fate, you can never be 100 percent sure when or even if the card will arrive. Send enough postcards and you stop worrying about it. (I sent one card from Australia that didn't reach Toby and Margot for a month or so. I took perverse comfort in that: Delayed gratification turns out to be sweeter, and I liked the idea that a secret clone of myself appeared to have camped out for weeks on Bondi Beach in Australia.)

Doing this on a daily basis had unexpected benefits. The missives made me feel closer to loved ones, yes, but the centering quality of sitting down and shutting off the phone and scrawling a few lines of free-associative self-analysis started to bolster my own emotional equilibrium too. Being on the road can get lonely, and mindlessly scrolling through your phone has a way of amplifying the feeling, but these experiments in writing with a pen seemed to settle my anxieties like shorthand (or longhand) therapy.

Maybe you've heard of the Slow Food movement, which has in part inspired people to celebrate the patience required to grow, harvest, cook, and eat food the way nature intended. Well, postcards are like Slow Texts. You express a thought to someone you care about, and that thought doesn't register on the other side for days, but the fact that you have forsaken the immediacy and disposability of the DM allows you to leave a more lasting imprint. In this era of broadcasting your feelings to the world via Facebook and Twitter and Instagram, there is something satisfying about the privacy of a postcard. It's from me to you—no one else—and even when it feels tossed off, it depends on a series of steps (writing, addressing, stamping) that layer the gesture with extra meaning.

As with Slow Food, though, you can't enjoy the good stuff without putting in extra work. Sending postcards—or making a sustained practice of sending postcards—requires preparation, supplies, and an unexpected degree of ingenuity. First off, you need pens. (I love the flow you get from an ultra-fine-point Sharpie.) It helps to maintain a stash of backup implements, just as it helps to tote around a new sheet of 35-cent postcard stamps. If you geek out as utterly as I do, you'll affix the stamps to the cards ahead of time so they're always ready for an impulsive mail drop. Speaking of which, should you find yourself far away from a familiar neighborhood, you'll have to track down a mailbox. Finding one in this digital era can be a more bewildering quest than you might imagine. (Pittsburgh seems to have plenty. Houston left me drenched in sweat as I walked for blocks and blocks in the summer heat hunting for a slot to slide a few notes into.)

Is the effort worth it? Put it this way: Right now I am writing this essay in my daughter Margot's room, and I see the evidence taped to her walls. There's the Bob Marley postcard I once sent her, and the David Byrne one. Our texted exchanges have vanished forever, but these cards remain. I need no further acknowledgment than that. Writing and sending postcards to the people I love has taught me that there is much to be gained from the practice of deliberateness.

Yes, you can text with anyone at any moment. But set aside a modest block of time—on a plane when the Wi-Fi doesn't work, at a table while you wait for a less-than-punctual dining companion—and you might discover, as I have, that there is a great deal to gain from the casual but concentrated enterprise of jotting down three or four sentences by hand.

How can I be sure? Well, Lauren lives with me now. We're married and we have baby twins, Jasper and Wesley. I proposed to her at Via Carota, our favorite restaurant in New York City, by sliding a postcard across the wooden table. One side of the card had an Art Deco illustration of the Manhattan skyline. On the other side I asked her to marry me. Postcards may be small and flimsy, but don't underestimate their power. She said *yes*.

"Postcards" originally appeared in *Real Simple* magazine.

About the Authors

Kevin Ashton is a technologist and author. He coined the term "the Internet of Things," co-founded the Auto-ID Center at the Massachusetts Institute of Technology, and his first book, *How to Fly a Horse: The Secret History of Creation, Invention, and Discovery*, was named Porchlight Business Book of the Year for 2015. He has also written for the *New York Times*, *The Atlantic*, *The Daily Telegraph*, and *Politico*. He is currently working on his second book, which explores how China changed television and television changed China.

Russell Banks is the internationally acclaimed author of eighteen works of fiction, including the novels *Continental Drift*, *Rule of the Bone*, *The Book of Jamaica* and *Lost Memory of Skin*, six short story collections, and several works of non-fiction, most recently *Voyager: Travel Writings*. Two of his novels, *The Sweet Hereafter* and *Affliction*, have been adapted into award-winning films. Banks has been a Pulitzer Prize Finalist (*Continental Drift, Cloudsplitter*) and a PEN/Faulkner Finalist (*Affliction, Cloudsplitter, Lost Memory of Skin*). His work has received numerous other awards, and has been widely translated and anthologized. Banks lives in upstate New York with his wife, the poet Chase Twichell.

Peter Behrens' first novel *The Law of Dreams* won the Governor General's Literary Award, Canada's top book prize. The New York Times hailed his second novel, *The O'Briens* as "a major accomplishment." His 2016 novel *Carry Me* was one of National Public Radio's *Best Reads of 2016*. Behrens was a 2015-16 Fellow of Harvard University's Radcliffe Institute for Advanced Study.

Madison Smartt Bell is the author of twelve novels, including *The Washington Square Ensemble*; *Waiting for the End of the World*; *Straight Cut*; *The Year of Silence*; *Soldier's Joy*; *Doctor Sleep*; *Save Me, Joe Louis*; *Ten Indians*; *Master of the Crossroads*; and *The Stone That the Builder Refused*. Bell has also published three collections of short stories: *Zero db*, *Barking Man*, and *Zig-Zag*. Bell's eighth novel, *All Souls' Rising*, was a finalist for the 1995 National Book Award and the 1996 PEN/Faulkner Award. His most recent novel is *Behind the Moon*.

Melissa Broder is a poet and writer. Her work includes the novel *The Pisces*, the poetry collection *Last Sext* and essay collection *So Sad Today*, as well as a popular Twitter feed—also titled *So Sad Today*—on which the book is based.

Wesley Brown is the author of three published novels, a collection of short stories and four produced plays, including *Dark Meat on a Funny Mind*. He wrote the narration for a segment of the 1997 PBS documentary, *W.E.B. Du Bois: A Biography in Four Voices*. He currently teaches literature, drama and creative writing at Bard College at Simon's Rock. He lives in Great Barrington, MA.

Charles Coe is the author of three books of poetry: *All Sins Forgiven: Poems for my Parents*, *Picnic on the Moon*, and *Memento Mori*, all published by Leapfrog Press. His novella *Spin Cycles*, about a homeless man living on the street in Boston, was published by Gemma Media. Charles is the recipient of fellowships from the Massachusetts Cultural Council and the St. Botolph Club of Boston, and was designated a "Boston Literary Light" by the Associates of the Boston Public Library. As a 2017 Artist-in-Residence for the city of Boston, he created an oral history project featuring residents of the Mission Hill neighborhood. Charles is adjunct professor of English with the Newport MFA program at Salve Regina University, where he teaches poetry and nonfiction.

Castle Freeman, Jr. was born in Texas, then raised and educated in Chicago, New York, and Philadelphia. He came to southeastern Vermont with his wife, Alice, on a whim and is still there forty-seven years later. He is the author of seven novels, more than fifty published short stories, two story collections, and more than one hundred essays as well as historical articles, op-ed matter, journalism, nature writing, and other nonfiction. Most of his writing brings to life the rural nature of Vermont and its people. Castle's most recently published novel is *The Devil in the Valley* (Overlook Press, NY, 2016).

Jeff Gordinier is the author of *Hungry: Eating, Road-Tripping, and Risking It All with the Greatest Chef in the World.* He lives close to the Hudson River with his wife, Lauren Fonda, and his four children.

Elizabeth Graver is the author of four novels, most recently *The End of the Point.* Her short fiction has been included in *Best American Short Stories, The Pushcart Prize Anthology* and *Prize Stories: The O. Henry Awards.*

Dan Grote is a formerly incarcerated writer who has gone from penning holdup notes to vigorously scribbling a happier ending to his story. You can find out more about him at his blog, www.freshfromthecan.blogspot.com.

Nikolai Grozni is the author of six books of fiction and one memoir. His work has appeared in *The Guardian, Harper's Magazine, The New York Times,* and many others.

Lewis Hyde is a poet, essayist, translator, and cultural critic with a particular interest in the public life of the imagination. His 1983 book, *The Gift*, illuminates and defends the non-commercial portion of artistic practice. *Trickster Makes This World* (1998) uses a group of ancient myths to argue for the disruptive intelligence that all cultures need if they are to remain lively and open to change. *Common as Air* (2010) is a spirited defense of our "cultural commons," that vast store of ideas, inventions, and works of art that we have inherited from the past and continue to enrich in the present. Hyde's most recent book, *A Primer for Forgetting*, explores the many situations in which forgetfulness is more useful than memory—in myth, personal psychology, politics, art, and spiritual life. A MacArthur Fellow and former director of undergraduate creative writing at Harvard University, Hyde taught creative writing and American literature for many years at Kenyon College.

Gabino Iglesias is a writer, professor, editor, and book reviewer living in Austin, Texas. His work has been translated into four languages, optioned for film, and nominated for the Wonderland Book Award, the Bram Stoker Award, and the Locus.

Pagan Kennedy tells stories about iconoclasts, humanitarian inventors, and scientific visionaries. Her eleven books include *The First Man-Made Man*, a study of the transgender pioneer Michael Dillon. Kennedy's journalism has appeared in dozens of publications including *The New York Times Magazine*, where she wrote the "Who Made That?" column. In the 1980s and '90s, she created a 'zine called *Pagan's Head* that anticipated today's self-produced samizdat—and was named the Queen of 'Zines by *Wired Magazine*. She is now a contributing writer for *The New York Times* Opinion section; she is also co-producing a serial podcast for the Radiotopia network.

John Kuntz is a playwright, actor, director, and solo performer. He is the author of more than 15 full-length plays including *Necessary Monsters*, *The Hotel Nepenthe* (published by Concord Free Press), *Starfuckers*, *Jasper Lake*, *The Annotated History of the American Muskrat*, *Sing Me To Sleep*, and *The Salt Girl*. He is the recipient of Elliot Norton Awards for Solo Performance (*Starfuckers*), Ensemble Work (*The Hotel Nepenthe*), Direction (*Blasted*) and two for Playwrighting (*The Hotel Nepenthe* and *The Salt Girl*), as well as many other awards. As an actor, he has worked with the Huntington, ART, Speakeasy, Lyric Stage, New Rep, and many other theater companies. He is a founding company member of the Actors' Shakespeare Project and an inaugural Playwrighting Fellow with the Huntington Theatre Company. He is currently a lecturer in Theatre, Dance and Media at Harvard University, an Associate Professor at The Boston Conservatory at Berklee, and the Artistic Director of the Derrah Theatre Lab.

Yiyun Li is a Chinese-American writer. Her short stories and novels have won several awards and distinctions, including the PEN/Hemingway Award and Guardian First Book Award for *A Thousand Years of Good Prayers*.

Alan Lightman is a physicist, writer, and professor of the practice of the humanities at MIT. His novel *Einstein's Dreams* was an international bestseller. His novel *The Diagnosis* was a finalist for the National Book Award. His essays have appeared in the *Atlantic, Granta, Harper's,* the *New Yorker,* the *New York Review of Books, Salon,* and other publications.

John Lilly was born in Chicago, attended high school in Cincinnati, and received an AB from Harvard College. His work history includes a stint with Richard Meier + Partners in Los Angeles and co-founding and operating a bookselling business in Scville, Spain. He lives in Manhattan with his wife and two children.

Stephen McCauley is the author of *My Ex-Life* and eight other novels. He is Co-Director of Creative Writing at Brandeis University.

Gregory Maguire is the author of *Wicked*, which inspired the Broadway musical of the same name, and ten other novels for adults, as well as about thirty books for children. His most recent titles are *Hiddensee*, for adults, and *Egg & Spoon*, for children.

Karan Mahajan is the author of *Family Planning* (Harper Perennial, 2008), an international Dylan Thomas Prize finalist; and *The Association of Small Bombs* (Viking, 2016), winner of the 2017 New York Public Library Young Lions Fiction Award that was named one of the *New York Times Book Review*'s "Ten Best Books of 2016" and shortlisted for the 2016 National Book Award. In 2017, *Granta* named him one of the Best Young American Novelists. His work has appeared in the *New York Times*, the New Yorker.com, and the *New Republic*.

Craig Moodie lives with his wife in Massachusetts. His work includes *A Sailor's Valentine and Other Stories*, *Salt Luck*, and, as John Macfarlane, the middle-grade novel *Stormstruck!*, a Kirkus Best Book. His fiction and essays have appeared in *On the Seawall*, *Sentence*, *SAIL*, *Good Old Boat*, and other publications.

Mary Norris is a writer and editor who lives in New York City. Originally from Cleveland, she was educated at Rutgers University, in New Jersey, and at the University of Vermont. Her first book, the *New York Times* best-selling *Between You and Me: Confessions of a Comma Queen* (Norton, 2015), was about her day job at *The New Yorker*, where she worked for more than thirty years as a copy editor. Her latest book, *Greek to Me: Adventures of the Comma Queen* (Norton, 2019), is about what she did in her spare time: study Greek, travel in Greece, read the classics, and otherwise cultivate life as a philhellene.

Joyce Carol Oates is the author of, most recently, the novels *My Life as a Rat* and *Pursuit*. Her most recent story collection is *Beautiful Days*. She is the 2019 recipient of the Jerusalem Prize and is currently Visiting Distinguished Writer in the Graduate Writing Program at New York University. Since 1978, she has been a member of the American Academy of Arts and Letters.

Ann Patchett is the author of eight novels and three works of nonfiction. Her latest novel is *The Dutch House*. She is the co-owner of Parnassus Books in Nashville, Tennessee.

Jordy Rosenberg is a transgender writer and scholar. He is an associate professor at the University of Massachusetts Amherst, where he teaches eighteenth-century literature and gender and sexuality studies. He has received fellowships and awards from the Marion and Jasper Whiting Foundation, the Ahmanson Foundation/J. Paul Getty Trust, the UCLA Center for 17th- and 18th-Century Studies, the Society for the Humanities at Cornell University, and the Clarion Foundation's Science Fiction and Fantasy Writers' Workshop. He is the author of a scholarly monograph, *Critical Enthusiasm: Capital Accumulation and the Transformation of Religious Passion*. He lives in New York City and Northampton, Massachusetts.

Elizabeth Spires is the author of seven collections of poetry, most recently *A Memory of the Future*, a *New York Times* Best Poetry Book of 2018. She has also written seven books for children, including *The Mouse of Amherst*, the tale of a white mouse who lives in Emily Dickinson's bedroom. She lives in Baltimore and teaches at Goucher College.

Elizabeth Wurtzel is a Downtown diva.

Concord Free Press is an ongoing experiment in publishing and community.

And now you're part of it.

This copy of *Concord Free Press Presents* is free. All we ask is that you give money to a group you support or someone in need. Where and how much you give—that's completely up to you. Just chart your donation at www.concordfreepress. com. Then pass your book along to another reader so that the giving can continue.

Concord Free Press is about inspiring generosity. Thanks so much for yours.

Please sign your copy of *Concord Free Press Presents* before you pass it on:

NAME	LOCATION
1.	
2.	
3.	
4.	
5.	
6.	
7.	
8.	
9.	
10.	

NAME	LOCATION

11.

12.

13.

14.

15.

16.

17.

18.

19.

20.

Concord Free Press

Editor-in-Chief
Stona Fitch

Fiction Editor
Ann Fitch

Poetry Editor
Ron Slate

Design Director
Chris DeFrancesco

Design and Production
Lynn Landry

Editorial Supervision
Robert Kelly

Associate Editor
Julia Cabiness Shivers

Publicity
Tanya Farrell
Wunderkind PR

Advisory Board
Megan Abbott
Russell Banks
Madison Smartt Bell
Hamilton Fish
Ron Koltnow
Gregory Maguire
William Martin
Stephen McCauley
John Netzer
Joyce Carol Oates
Tom Perrotta
Scott Phillips
Francine Prose
Sebastian Stuart
Paul Tremblay

Printing of this book was subsidized by a generous donation from **Harvest** in New York City. (www.getharvest.com)

Other Books from the Concord Free Press

Another Way to Fall
Brian Evenson and
Paul Tremblay

About the House
Jenny and Ron Slate
(illustrated by Karl Stevens)

Five Things I Know
Reverend Kim K. Crawford

IOU
Edited by Ron Slate

The Rockaways
Edited by Hamilton Fish, photos
by Gilles Peress

Zig Zag
Madison Smartt Bell

Round Mountain
Castle Freeman, Jr.

A Handbook of American Prayer
Lucius Shepard
(introduction by Russell Banks)

Rut
Scott Phillips

The Next Queen of Heaven
Gregory Maguire

Push Comes to Shove
Wesley Brown

Give + Take
Stona Fitch

CONCORD
FREE
PRESS